HIS
MILLIONAIRE
MAID

COLEEN KWAN

Entangled Publishing, LLC
2614 South Timberline Road
Suite 109
Fort Collins, CO 80525
Visit our website at www.entangledpublishing.com.

Lovestruck is an imprint of Entangled Publishing, LLC.

Edited by Stacy Abrams and Lydia Sharp
Cover design by Heather Howland
Cover art by iStock

Manufactured in the United States of America

First Edition July 2015

To my family.

Chapter One

"My life sucks," Nina Beaumont declared, glaring at the road ahead of her, hands clenched around the steering wheel of her BMW.

A snort came from her cell phone mounted in its hands-free cradle. "Yeah, right," her best friend, Lindsey, said. "It sucks to have a megamillionaire daddy like Carson Beaumont. I'm sure most of America can sympathize with that."

"Most of America doesn't know how difficult it is working for that megamillionaire daddy."

"Come on, Nina. After all the clashes between you two, your dad's just relieved you're finally working for him."

Nina blew out a sigh. "But if I wasn't working for him, I wouldn't be in this mess."

"What kind of mess?"

"A horrible, never-saw-this-coming kind of mess." Nina chewed on her lip. "It's just hit me out of nowhere…and now I don't know how I'm going to face everyone at the office when I get back to San Francisco—"

Her voice broke up, and a lump formed in her throat. Damn it, why did this have to happen now? Why did being a Beaumont continue to screw with her life?

"Nina?" Concern threaded Lindsey's voice. "You sound really upset. Tell me what's going on."

Nina lifted her foot off the gas pedal and eased the car down to forty miles per hour. She was cruising through redwood forests and rolling pastures with the ocean sparkling in the near distance—gorgeous countryside she barely noticed. She was also headed in the complete opposite direction of where she was supposed to be—and wasn't that an apt metaphor for her entire life? Instead of heading south toward San Francisco, she was going north, winding through Mendocino County, not with any specific destination in mind but because the thought of returning to Beaumont, Inc. headquarters and facing the work colleagues she'd thought were her friends made her feel sick to her stomach.

"I came up to Sonoma yesterday," she said. Beaumont, Inc. owned a string of exclusive upmarket golf resorts, and she'd gone to the one in Sonoma County for a human resources meeting, an ordinary gathering about work policies. "And this morning before I left, Harry, my manager, called to tell me I got a promotion—"

"But that's fantastic news!" Lindsey interrupted. "You never told me you were in line for a promotion."

"Well, I never thought I'd be chosen. I was so stunned I was speechless."

"You, speechless? I find that hard to believe. So what's the problem?"

"In all the confusion, I forgot I had some questions for

Harry. So I called him back. But an intern answered, and when she went to look for him, instead of putting me on hold, she left the phone on her desk." Nina sucked in a deep breath. "And I overheard a couple of people talking about me."

"Oh, no. I'm guessing it wasn't anything good?"

"They were talking about my promotion, and they both agreed that no one else stood a chance against me, no matter how hard they worked, because I'm a fricking Beaumont." She heard the bitterness in her voice but couldn't suppress it. "Can you believe it? Doesn't matter if I deserved the promotion or not—everyone assumes I only got it because my daddy owns the company."

"You work hard; you don't trade on your name. You shouldn't listen to idle gossip."

Nina shook her head. "This was Ryan and Fiona talking. We've worked late nights together, gone out for Friday night drinks, talked about ourselves. I thought we were *friends.*" Her heart panged. That was the worst part, finding out they had never really been friends and could never be friends because of who she was—a Beaumont heiress.

She should be used to it by now. Lindsey was her only true friend. They'd met in college when Nina was going through her rebellious stage, rejecting her family and trying to embarrass them. Lindsey had always supported her, even at her brattiest worst. But even she couldn't fully understand the unique torments Nina suffered.

"If they say things like that behind your back, then you're better off without them," Lindsey said.

The problem wasn't just with Ryan and Fiona, though. She had never fit in with the other rich kids at the exclusive school her father had insisted she attend. She'd gone out of her way to mix with ordinary people, but there'd always been a change in their attitude—subtle or otherwise—when they learned who she was. She'd become sensitized to that, hyperaware that being rich—and obscenely rich at that—affected people's perception of her. Affected how they treated her. She was never sure what people really thought of her.

Like Oliver, her ex. After many dating disasters, she'd thought she'd finally found a man who loved her for herself, only to discover he was more in love with her trust fund. The memory caused the fist around her heart to clench even tighter. Six months after their breakup, his betrayal still hurt.

"Damn it," she blurted. "For once in my life I'd like to live somewhere where no one knows who I am, without my money or my last name to screw things up."

There was a pause on the other end of the call before Lindsey said, "Oh, honey, that's a nice idea, but you wouldn't last more than two months."

"Is that what you think?" Nina took the next curve in the road a tad too fast, causing her to tap on the brakes as she negotiated this twisty section of the highway. "You're supposed to be on my side."

"I am, and I love you, but let's be serious. You might have been a rebel a few years ago, but you're past that stage. You're wiser now, and since you went to work for your dad you've—dare I say it—gotten used to a cushier lifestyle. I bet you're cruising in your swanky BMW right now, wearing designer jeans and sunglasses. Am I right or am I right?"

Nina shifted guiltily in her leather seat. "Okay, yeah. But the BMW was a gift from my dad. I'd never have bought a car like this. And as for these jeans, you talked me into them, and—" She let out a groan. "Oh, Lindsey. How did I end up like this? Where did I go wrong? Remember college? We used to shop at thrift stores and hitchhike and survive on ramen noodles."

"*You* were trying to stick it to your father, but *I* had no choice," Lindsey pointed out. "And, frankly, I don't miss those days. I'm doing great now, and I enjoy spending the money I've earned."

Unlike Nina, Lindsey had graduated from college with honors, was a rising star at her publishing company, and had a nice, steady boyfriend. Lindsey's life was on the up and up, whereas Nina's seemed to hit one dead end after another.

"I'm not trying to stick it to my dad anymore."

A year and a half ago, she'd become mixed up with a group of hard-core radicals, but when their protest at an economic forum had turned violent, she'd realized she didn't share their nihilist views. But by then she'd already been arrested, caught up with the other glass-smashing thugs. Her father and his high-powered attorney had gotten her out of serious trouble, and she knew that she owed him. That was why she'd finally agreed to come on board at Beaumont, Inc.—to mend things between her and her dad. At the time it had seemed like a good, sensible decision for once in her life, but now she wasn't sure about anything.

"The thing is, I'm sick of how my life is panning out. I'm sick of being Nina Beaumont. I can never get away from her. In fact, I should just stop in the nearest town"—she peered at a signpost indicating the next town was a place called Hartley—"and go incognito for a month or so."

Lindsey chuckled. "Do it, then. I dare you."

"I'm serious!"

"Yeah, okay, I'll humor you for a little while. So if you

did go incognito, what about your job? Are you just going to resign in a fit?"

"No," Nina said, thinking rapidly. "But I'm due to take some vacation time starting next week anyway, so no one will miss me for at least three weeks. After that I can arrange something with Dad, depending on how it goes."

"You really shouldn't waste your vacation on a wacky scheme like this. Your dad has a house in Hawaii, doesn't he? Why don't you go there and catch some sun? You'll feel heaps better."

"You don't think I can do this?"

"Oh, I think you're capable of anything." There was no mistaking the amusement in Lindsey's voice.

Nina pressed her lips together. If her best friend and biggest supporter didn't take her seriously, then how would she ever break free? She firmed her grip on the wheel as she approached another bend. Afternoon sunlight flashed through tall trees, temporarily blinding her. She eased the car around the corner, squinting against the glare, only to find herself barreling straight toward a fat brown duck waddling across the road.

"Shit!"

She slammed on the brakes, instinctively veering away from the bird. The duck squawked and took off across the windshield, blocking her view. Tires squealed, and Nina screamed as the car skidded off the road before hurtling down a steep embankment. For several heart-stopping seconds, everything was a blur of whipping greenery, and then she was out in the open, heading straight for...a large pit filled with still black water.

Holy crap on a cracker. There was no time to think, let

alone scream. With a huge splash, the car torpedoed into the water, and the air bag exploded in her face. *Get out, get out, get out!* her brain shrieked at her. The air bag deflated in her lap. She unbuckled her seat belt and instinctively grabbed her phone. Her tote bag had fallen to the floor. She bent to retrieve it, but the car tilted forward and slid deeper into the water.

Panic ruptured in her, but then she remembered an episode of *Mythbusters* she'd seen about what to do in this kind of situation and pressed the button to open her window. As water rushed into the car, accelerating its descent, she ordered herself to stay calm. She pulled herself through the window, kicked away from the sinking car, then splashed and spluttered to the shoreline. Panting, she dragged herself onto the weed-infested bank and watched as her car slowly disappeared beneath the surface.

"Nina? Nina? Talk to me, for God's sakes."

Incredibly, Lindsey was still on the phone, thanks to the wonders of state-of-the-art water-resistant technology. In a daze, Nina lifted the cell to her ear.

"I'm fine," she said, thrusting her fingers through her soaked hair. "Just had a little, um, accident." She picked a slimy bit of vegetation out of her hair and flicked it away.

"What! Are you hurt? What happened…"

Lindsey's barrage of questions floated over Nina's head as she watched bubbles popping on the surface, marking the watery grave of her BMW. Her car had sunk into what appeared to be a disused quarry. The water was deep and still, and her car had disappeared, leaving behind no trace except for a few skid marks.

"My car's totaled, but I'm okay." She flexed various muscles and squinted at herself. She was soaked but apparently unscathed.

"Don't move," Lindsey ordered. "I'm going to call your dad right now. He'll come out and rescue you."

Lindsey's words pierced Nina's daze. "No! Don't do that. Don't tell him anything."

"Why not? He'll be so worried about you. He won't care if you've wrecked the BMW. He'll just buy you another one."

That was *exactly* what he'd do, and then she'd be right back where she started. She'd be rebellious little Nina again, but this time with a reputation for crashing expensive cars and wasting people's time. No, she couldn't stay on this hamster wheel for the rest of her life. She had to make a stand for herself, and right now was the perfect moment to start fresh.

Her car had sunk, taking everything with it. All she had now was her phone, the soaked clothes on her back, and a few dollars in her jeans pocket. No BMW, no fancy wardrobe, no credit cards, and most important of all, *no identity*. She was Ms. Nobody from Nowheresville. Just like she'd said she wanted not five minutes ago. Maybe fate had been listening to her after all.

"I think there's a reason I crashed my car here," she said to Lindsey. "This is my chance to find out what it's like *not* to be me."

• • •

Nina found a house about half a mile from the quarry, and it appeared no one was home. She crouched behind the bushes, rubbing her chilled arms. On the clothesline nearby flapped some women's clothing—cheap, plain, chain store clothing—that looked about her size. She needed to change out of her clothes, not only because they were wet, but because the pricey labels would give her away if she was serious about going incognito.

Of course she was serious. To prove it to herself, she whipped out her cell phone and called her manager. She told him something unexpected had come up and she wouldn't make it to the office this afternoon and needed tomorrow off, too. Harry didn't make a big deal about it. After tomorrow, she was on vacation anyway, and there wasn't anything urgent waiting for her at the office. Then again, Harry never reprimanded her, even when she made mistakes—because she was Carson Beaumont's daughter.

"Harry," she said, putting on a casual tone. "Just out of curiosity, why did you give me the promotion and not someone else like Ryan or Fiona?"

"Because you're the most qualified, of course." Harry gave a hearty, fake-sounding laugh that confirmed Nina's worst fears. She wasn't the best qualified, and Harry didn't honestly believe she deserved the promotion. He was only doing it to impress the higher-ups, or because he'd been ordered to.

"I see. Okay. Well, thanks." She couldn't even pretend to be pleased, she was so nauseated, and quickly ended the call.

The sorry truth was, although she worked harder than her colleagues, she'd never pushed for that promotion because her heart wasn't truly in her job. She'd taken it to mend fences with her dad, but now this promotion meant she was stuck there for the long haul.

Okay, that did it. She was even more determined to follow through with this screwball plan of hers.

After another quick scan of the deserted yard, she darted

forward and snatched a few bits of clothing off the line before scampering back to the bushes. Her heart pumped with nervousness as she stripped and changed into faded jeans, a cheap T-shirt, and a scruffy denim jacket. She would leave her designer jeans and T-shirt hanging on the line for the owner; that would more than cover the cost of these Kmart threads.

The only clue to her former life lay in her striking, hand-tooled cowboy boots, now soggy and squelchy and uncomfortable. But she had no way of replacing them, so she'd just have to make do.

When she was fully clothed, she couldn't resist taking a selfie and sending it to Lindsey. Lindsey clearly thought she was nuts, but she was used to Nina's schemes by now, and she'd keep her secret.

She slipped the phone into her pocket, squared her shoulders, and stared at the road leading into Hartley, a place she'd never heard of. A place where she could be herself. Who knew what lay ahead for her? It could be disaster, embarrassment, or total failure. But she had to find out. Going back wasn't an option anymore.

With fingers crossed, she took the first steps toward her new identity.

. . .

Joe Farina sat back on his heels and rolled his shoulders, trying to ease the tension knotting his back. Some days, owning and running the Comet Inn was tough on a guy, and this was one of those days. One of the waitstaff had twisted an ankle, his chef was threatening to cut someone's balls off, and the new temporary employee who was supposed to have arrived at two still hadn't turned up. It was now after five, and since he was short staffed, he was on his hands and knees in the reception lobby cleaning up a bottle of lavender oil one of the guests had spilled.

The front door jingled as someone entered the inn. Joe stood and his gaze fell on a girl who didn't look a day over eighteen. She was small and slim, with short blond hair and blue eyes almost too big for her face, like a doll. Judging by her faded jeans, cheap T-shirt, and scruffy denim jacket, she had to be the new temp.

"You're here. Finally." He couldn't temper the frustration in his voice.

The girl stopped and raised her eyebrows. "Excuse me?"

He strode forward, his mind leaping ahead to everything that still needed doing. "I'm Joe Farina, your new boss. You're the temp I've been waiting for all afternoon."

Her eyes widened as they fixed on his hands. Joe paused. He'd forgotten about the rubber gloves he was wearing. Big, blinding, flamingo-pink gloves. Damn.

She bit her lip as if trying not to smile. "Cute. Pink suits you."

He tore off the gloves and tossed them next to his bucket, feeling strangely flustered. "I'm allergic to lavender," he said stiffly. "And those were the only gloves I could find." Why did he need to explain himself to her? "You are my new maid, right?"

She tugged at her jacket. "Uh…your new maid…yeah. Right."

Joe bit back a groan. She wasn't slow-witted, was she? She didn't look slow-witted. Her eyes were deep blue and curious as she glanced between him and the reception area. Her stance was wary, as if she wasn't sure she should be here.

He waved a hand impatiently. "You were supposed to be here at two. I can't have employees who turn up late, especially on their first day."

She jutted her chin as if ready to argue with him. "I'm not—" She stopped abruptly, looking conflicted.

A beat of silence passed as they sized each other up. At first glance, he'd thought she was a teenager, but now that she was closer, he revised his estimate to early twenties, no more than twenty-five. Her hair was several shades of blonde, from ice to honey to caramel, and it was messy and slightly damp, as if she'd been swimming recently. Her mouth was wide and sensual, balancing out a stubborn chin. He liked what he saw, he realized, especially that bold curve to her jaw.

His gaze caught on a weird bit of green stuff tangled in her hair. Was that a fancy barrette? No, it looked more like some kind of vegetation.

"What?" She shifted uncomfortably. "Is there dirt on my face?"

"No, something in your hair." He reached out impulsively and snagged the damp piece out of her hair. "What is this? It looks like...duckweed?"

Her cheeks turned bright pink—almost as pink as his embarrassing gloves—as she snatched the sliver from his fingers. "No, it must have fallen off a tree, but thanks."

It was definitely duckweed, but clearly she wasn't going to tell him how it got in her hair, and he didn't have time for this.

"Listen. I'm really busy. If you want the job, then come

with me." He moved toward the hallway leading off the reception lobby, throwing a glance over his shoulder to see if she followed. When she did, his small twinge of relief surprised him. He was glad to get another pair of hands, but was he also glad it was her?

He led the way into the linen room and grabbed a stack of clean sheets and towels. He dumped them into her arms.

"Got that?"

Her eyes widened above the stack of linen, but she didn't complain, just nodded like she knew he was testing her. Okay, then. She'd passed.

He walked into an adjoining utility room filled with cleaning equipment.

"There are eight guest rooms that get dusted and cleaned every day, even when they're unoccupied. I like to keep them ready to use at all times."

He picked up a bucket filled with cleaning products and a mop. The temp shifted the pile of linen in her arms and waggled one hand at him. "I got that, too."

She had spunk, he'd give her that. Her sharp blue eyes dared him, so he handed the bucket and mop to her. She winced as she struggled to balance her load.

"Maybe I should—" Joe began.

"No, no. I can manage. It's the least I can do, seeing as I'm late."

This could be interesting. At the back of his mind a warning buzzer sounded. He needed someone efficient, not interesting.

But he couldn't resist gesturing at the hulking industrial-strength vacuum cleaner in the corner. "Think you can manage that, too?"

She gulped. "Uh, I might have to come back for it."

"Well, since it's your first day, I'll carry it for you."

He led the way upstairs and showed her into one of the vacant suites. The Lily room was light and bright, with blue-and-white wallpaper, a queen-size bed, a mirrored armoire, and a private balcony with stunning views of the Pacific coastline.

The temp set down her load with a sigh of relief before looking about her with interest. She ran her fingers over a maple dresser and nodded her approval before opening the door to the balcony and surveying the view.

"Pretty," she said.

Hartley wasn't a big town. From the balcony, they looked straight down the main street lined with stores and business-es. The street ended at the beach, and beyond that the ocean, now splashed with orange from a spectacular sunset.

"Nice little town you've got here," she said, sounding surprised.

She was acting more like a guest than a casual cleaner.

"Glad you approve," Joe retorted, not bothering to hide his sarcasm.

She blushed and hurried on, "I mean, it's so different from San Francisco."

"Is that where you're from?"

She hesitated before nodding.

"Well, don't go thinking things are slow around here just because it's quiet," he continued. "I don't allow laziness."

She frowned at him. "What makes you think I'm lazy?"

The blue glitter in her eyes sent a strange frisson down his spine. Christ, what was that sensation? Excitement?

"You're admiring the view instead of thinking about

your duties."

"I apologize. Please, let's get back to my *duties*." The corners of her lips curled up as if she were thinking of other duties she could perform for him.

Joe coughed. Her brief smile disappeared, and she pulled back her shoulders, but that only drew his attention to her breasts. She was small there, but that didn't stop his imagination from freewheeling, wondering what she looked like naked. Slender like a dancer, with firm, perky breasts — Damn it, what was wrong with him? Annoyed with himself, he gestured at the adjoining bathroom.

"Your first job is to change the linen and clean the bathroom here and next door. But before you do that, I'll take you through to the bar and restaurant and introduce you to the rest of the staff. Besides taking care of these rooms, you're expected to bus tables in the bar and help out in the kitchen. Tonight you're also on dish duty, since one of my kitchen hands is off."

She blinked and faltered back. "Wow…uh, okay…"

Joe narrowed his eyes on her fingers as she toyed nervously with a pricey silver necklace strung around her delicate throat. Despite the blue-collar clothes, she seemed too fragile for hard physical labor, which the job required.

"Look." He rested his hands on his hips, squaring his feet before her. "If you're not up to it, just say so. I won't hold it against you." Although he'd have a few words to say to the employment agency. They'd been having trouble supplying him with reliable staff lately, but this time they'd really screwed up.

His words seemed to have an electrifying effect on her. She drew herself up to her full height, which wasn't much.

"Who says I'm not up to it?" Her eyes almost spat with indignation. She was quite the fireball when she was riled. "I can handle a few bathrooms and clearing tables and washing dishes. I'm not some pampered rich kid with servants waiting on her hand and foot!"

He blinked at her outburst and bided his time until she'd calmed down.

"So," he said, folding his arms. "Who are you, then? You never told me your name."

• • •

Nina licked her lips that had suddenly dried at Joe's question. She'd had the answers all figured out in her head, but having Joe stare at her made her thoughts scatter like that damned duck on the road that had started this weird chain of events.

This Joe Farina guy was one of the tallest, biggest men she'd ever come across. He towered over her, but in a good way—good to look at, at any rate. His broad shoulders and lean hips were accentuated by a tight black T-shirt and close-fitting jeans. His hair was thick and dark and tousled, his eyes were the deepest mocha brown, and his movie-star looks were enough to make a girl swoon—even when he wore pink rubber gloves. Her knees weakened, a bead of perspiration breaking out between her breasts.

Crap, this was no time to get all steamed up over a man, especially a man she was about to lie to.

She tilted her chin up and returned his blunt stare. "You didn't give me a chance to introduce myself before you hustled me up here." She cleared her throat, praying she wouldn't stutter over her next words. "I'm Nina. Nina Summers."

She'd been christened Annette Martha, after her two grandmothers, but she'd always called herself Nina, and Summers was her late mother's maiden name. Half an hour ago, while walking into Hartley and concocting her cover story, she'd resolved not to stray too far from the truth. She was Nina Summers from San Francisco, a down-on-her-luck girl hoping to make a fresh start in a seaside community. She'd entered the Comet Inn hoping for information on possible employment in the area; she hadn't expected to walk straight into a job, albeit on false pretenses.

Joe stuck his hand out. "Pleased to meet you, Nina. Sorry I hurried you in without a formal introduction. I'm Joe Farina," he repeated, "owner of the Comet Inn."

The unexpected thaw in his manner threw her, and when she clasped his hand, her wits were further confused by the sudden seductive warmth of his callused palm. Holy hell, this man had some kind of magic touch. For a few moments all she could think about was his hands drifting over her, heating her skin, pleasuring her senses.

She hurriedly pulled her hand away. "Farina? That's Italian, right?" she asked in an effort to mask her discomfort.

"Yeah. I'm told I get a little hot tempered at times, so be warned."

His mouth lifted in a quirky little smile that sent a tingle down to her toes. She groaned silently. Why did he have such a killer smile? Why him, the first person she had to convince of her new identity? If she couldn't get past Joe's guard, then she might as well give up right now.

"I don't mind a hot temper." She flicked her fingers through her hair. "I can get hot tempered myself sometimes."

His eyebrows lifted, and the air between them quivered

with an unmistakable spark, a sharp tug of mutual attraction. Joe must have felt it, too, because he stepped back, looking momentarily confused.

"Uh—" He cleared his throat. "Let's go downstairs and do the paperwork so you can start on those guest rooms."

Darn, she shouldn't have done that hair-flicking thing. What was wrong with her? Less than an hour into her new identity and already she couldn't help flirting with her sexy new boss. She really had to get a hold of herself if she wanted this to work. Biting her cheek, she followed Joe downstairs and along a passageway that led to the back of the building, which appeared to be a private section.

He led her to his office and took down her particulars.

"Got any ID on you?" he asked.

Back in college she'd had a fake ID in the name of Nina Summers, but she'd left that in San Francisco. She'd have to ask Lindsey to mail it to her.

She shook her head. "No, but I'll get it to you as soon as I can."

He nodded, wrote something, and then glanced back at her. "Where are you staying in town?"

"Oh." *Good question.* "I don't know. I just got in this afternoon."

"Yeah?" His eyes narrowed on her. "The agency must've interviewed you by phone if you've only just arrived in Hartley?"

"Uh-huh. I, er, caught the bus in." She pushed her hands into the pockets of her denim jacket.

"No luggage?"

She'd prepared for that question. "I feel a bit stupid," she said, lifting her shoulders in a self-deprecating manner.

"I fell asleep on the bus, and when I woke up all my stuff had disappeared. I made the bus driver stop and search the bus, but the thief must have already gotten off, because we couldn't find anything, and by that time some of the passengers were upset with me for making them late."

Joe let out a soft whistle. "That's a lousy way to arrive in town." He looked her over again. "So that's all you have with you? Not even a purse?"

"Not even a purse. That's why I can't show you any ID. All I have is my phone and a few dollars in my back pocket. I don't suppose there's a youth hostel around here?"

"Not in Hartley." He riffled his hair and sighed. "Look, there's a room next door you can have. It's nothing fancy, but I won't charge you for it until you're back on your feet."

She lit up, surprised and touched by his offer. "Oh, that would be fantastic! Thank you, that's really generous of you."

Good-looking *and* kind to strangers. Joe was pretty awesome. But, more importantly, she now had a job *and* a place to stay. That wasn't so hard. Things were looking up.

"You don't happen to have a universal phone charger, too, do you?" she asked. "The jerk took everything."

"Sure, we keep a few spare for guests." He rummaged in his desk drawer and handed her a charger.

"Thanks." She sighed in gratitude. "You're a lifesaver."

He shrugged. "Let me show you your room."

Joe led her out of his office and back into the corridor. "Like I said, it's nothing fancy. No en suite, but there's a bathroom down the hall—not renovated like the others but usable. And you don't have to worry about guests here, because this section of the inn isn't for public use." He opened the neighboring door and gestured her to go in. "No one's used this room in a while."

Nina walked into the room and stopped dead. God, he hadn't been kidding when he said it wasn't fancy. Dull gray walls, scuffed floorboards, a single bed, a scratched desk, and a sagging armchair. A narrow window looked out on the service yard where the trash bins were kept. No private balcony. No stunning beachfront view. The room was clean and habitable, but about as welcoming as a prison cell, and a million miles away from her bright, comfy apartment back in the city.

As she looked around, Joe's gaze zeroed in on her. He was waiting for her reaction. Maybe he expected her to complain. She took a breath, searching for something positive to say, but failed.

"Well, okay," she muttered.

Joe stepped forward. She sensed him weighing her up. "Is there a problem?"

No problem at all. Except her car was at the bottom of a quarry, she had fewer friends than she'd assumed, and she was diving headfirst into her craziest scheme ever. A sense of loneliness hit her, making her shiver, but she pushed away the vulnerability.

"It's been a long day." She shrugged.

He didn't speak for a while, and the silence crackled with tension.

"Are you in trouble with the law?" he asked, his voice surprisingly gentle.

"What? N-no!" she spluttered. He sensed something didn't add up, she realized, and she had to give him a plausible story. "I'm not running from the police. It's more of a...a family issue. I had to get away for a while, and this job came up…" She silently prayed that whoever had really been sent to this job would never turn up. "I'll admit I don't have much experience cleaning or busing tables, but I'm a fast learner. Please, I could use a break."

And Joe was a good guy. Even though she'd only met him half an hour ago, there was something intrinsically trustworthy about him.

He studied her a moment more and then released a sigh. "I might regret this later, but okay, I'll give you a chance."

She grinned at him, unable to hold back her relief. "Thank you. I won't let you down."

"You'd better not. I don't have time for games."

"Doesn't that depend on the game and who's playing?" Her smile widened.

Joe blinked at her, and that spark between them was back, flashing in the air, too obvious to miss.

"Uh, yeah." He coughed, shifted on his feet. "Well, you're welcome to this room for as long as you need it. Linen and blankets are in the supply room. And like I said, bathroom's down the hall. Come on, I'll show you around the bar and introduce you to the rest of the staff."

He walked out, leaving Nina to stare after him. He really had the cutest ass in those tight jeans. She couldn't stop smiling. Joe had no idea who she was. She had flirted with him with impunity, and her name and wealth had nothing to do with his reaction. Not that she was purposely going to flirt with him, though, because he was her employer and she wanted to make a good impression. But it didn't hurt that he was the hottest guy she'd come across in a long while. Not one bit.

Chapter Two

Beggars can't be choosers, Joe told himself. He needed a maid, and Nina was here, so he would let her stay. It all made sense. But deep down, he didn't feel sensible. He felt like an idiot. Because of *her*. Because of how she made him feel when she tipped those bright blue eyes and slanted that sexy, mischievous smile at him.

After all these years, he hadn't thought it possible that a woman could get him so hot and bothered, but Nina did something to him, got him doing and thinking crazy things, and he wasn't sure he liked that.

"So tell me more about the Comet Inn," Nina said as she caught up with him.

They were back in the reception lobby, and Joe paused to take in the cozy, wood-paneled interior. No matter how many times he saw this place, he always felt a thrill from knowing he was the owner. When he was fifteen, he'd gotten his first job here as a lowly kitchen hand; then five years ago, he'd bought the historic but dilapidated inn and worked his butt off bringing it up to scratch.

"As you can see, it's pretty old." He gestured at the timber beams and windows. "About a hundred years. Originally built to accommodate sailors, but we get most of our trade on weekends and vacations. Accommodation upstairs for eight couples. We don't do breakfast, but there's a good coffee shop on the corner. Nowadays most of our revenue comes from the bar and restaurant. We're open for dinner six nights a week, and the kitchen does a bar menu, too."

He led her through stained-glass doors into the bar, a spacious area with exposed brick walls, a long, polished counter, and French doors exposing the view to the courtyard.

Vince, his bartender and friend, nodded at him from behind the counter. "Hey, how did it go at the bank today?"

Joe shook his head. "Not so great. I'll fill you in later."

But Vince wasn't paying him much attention. His focus had slid past Joe and fastened on Nina. Joe gestured to her.

"Vince, meet Nina Summers. She's new in town and will be cleaning the rooms, busing tables, and helping out in the kitchen. Nina, this is Vince Nucifora, the guy in charge of the bar."

The bartender wiped his hand on a cloth before eagerly shaking hands with Nina.

"Hey, Nina. Welcome to Hartley and the Comet Inn." Vince winked at her. "You'll like it here, as long as you don't mind having a slave driver for a boss."

"A slave driver, huh? I never would have guessed." Nina peeked impishly at Joe.

She likes to tease, Joe thought, refusing to react. "I'll take you through to the kitchen and introduce you to Sarah."

When Joe had started turning a profit at the inn, he'd built an extension to house the restaurant and fitted out a brand-spanking-new kitchen. This was now the undisputed domain of Sarah Wainwright, his exacting, talented head chef. As they entered the kitchen, Sarah was complaining loudly, and when she spotted him, she marched over.

"Look at these." She thrust a handful of mushrooms in his face. "That Greg has some nerve, trying to pass this garbage on to me. They're not even good enough for soup. I'm going to call him right now and give him hell."

Joe didn't feel much sympathy for Greg. Every supplier to the restaurant knew Sarah's rigorous standards.

"Go ahead and call him," he said, "but first I'd like to introduce you to a new employee." He made the introductions. Unlike Vince, Sarah greeted Nina with some reserve.

"Have you worked in hospitality long?" Sarah asked, eyeing Nina's disheveled appearance.

Nina cleared her throat. "About eighteen months. I was waitressing down in San Francisco."

"Where in San Francisco?"

"A coffee shop," Nina said.

"Which one?"

Nina blinked nervously several times. "Uh, the, uh, Daily Grind. Good name for a coffee shop, huh?"

Sarah didn't let up. "And where in San Francisco is it?"

"Well, uh, it was in the Embarcadero, but it closed down a month ago."

"So you've never worked in a restaurant before?"

"No." Nina stood her ground. "But I'm eager to learn."

"Humph." Sarah aimed a look at Joe as if to say, *God, a newbie? What were you thinking!*

He said, "Nina will be busing tables tonight and helping with the dish washing, since Nathan's out of action."

"In those heels?" Sarah gestured at Nina's fancy cowboy boots. "You won't last an hour."

Nina's cheeks flushed as she lifted her chin. "I'll be fine."

Joe glanced at Nina's boots. They were definitely sexy, but also impractical, and the leather looked damp. He was about to explain that Nina's stuff had been stolen, but stopped himself, figuring she probably didn't want everyone knowing her personal problems.

Sarah all but rolled her eyes. "Don't say I didn't warn you."

Joe tugged at Nina's elbow. "You'll meet the rest of the staff when you come on duty. Right now, I need you to get moving on those guest rooms."

When they were out in the lobby, Nina turned to him. "Did I do something to annoy Sarah? I get the feeling she doesn't like me much."

But Vince likes you. The thought intruded into his mind without warning. Why did that bother him? Vince was a good friend. He was an easygoing guy who liked a lot of people—that was what made him such a good bartender.

"Sarah can be prickly," he said. "She's a perfectionist, but if you work hard and pull your weight, she'll come around."

Nina moved closer, near enough for him to see the faint dusting of freckles across her pert nose and the tiny pulse beating at the base of her throat. "I intend to, and I'm grateful to you for giving me a chance."

Joe's concentration drifted to her mouth, those soft pink lips inciting illicit thoughts. Hell, he'd like to give her something more than just a chance.

"Let's see how you do tonight," he said.

"Sure thing. Why don't I clean that up for a start?" She nodded at the remaining spilled lavender oil in the corner of the reception lobby. "I'm not allergic to lavender, so you can keep the pink gloves for yourself."

He ignored the quip. "That'd be great."

She drew in a deep breath and flexed her arms like she was about to run a race. "This is a new beginning for me."

"Yeah?" Once again his curiosity piqued. "You're turning over a new leaf or something?"

"Not only a new leaf—I'm turning over a whole tree."

"Well, just remember not to drop a load on me while you're doing all this turning."

"I won't, Joe. I promise. You won't regret hiring me."

Famous last words. Joe rubbed his upper lip as he watched her bend over the bucket he'd left in the lobby. The sight of her tight, round butt captivated him. Those boots of hers looked expensive, especially compared to the rest of her clothes. How could she afford them? Maybe she had a shoe fetish…aw, hell. Now he couldn't help picturing her wearing nothing but those boots.

• • •

Nina was ready to lose it. If Sarah told her one more time to move her ass, she was going to tip her fully laden bus pan over the chef's head.

Her feet, tortured by her boots, moaned in protest as she carried the full bus pan into the kitchen. Her shoulder muscles had stopped complaining an hour ago and were now numb, but she knew as soon as she sat down they'd start bitching again. It was better to keep moving. Also, staying on the move meant she was less likely to be the target of Sarah's ire.

Well, this was what she'd wanted, wasn't it? No special favors because of who she was. Yeah, now she knew what life was like on the other side. If she wasn't aching with exhaustion, she'd have to laugh at the irony.

Nina hefted the bus pan onto the counter where Trevor, the other kitchen hand, worked. In between clearing tables, she'd helped him rinse and wash, though she was a tortoise compared to him. And a clumsy one, too, as she'd broken two plates, the cost of which, Trevor had informed her, would be deducted from her pay.

"Is it always this busy on a Thursday night?" she asked, leaning against the counter to give her feet a break.

"Gets busier every month." Trevor kept on stacking dirty dishes as he talked. "Sarah's new menu is a hit. You gotta try her twice-cooked pork belly with lentils."

Nina groaned. "Stop talking about food. All I had was a burger and fries like twelve hours ago." It felt like twelve hours, though in reality less than three hours had passed since she'd been allowed to chow down a quick meal before the dinner service started. The burger had been very good. Since then she'd been working nonstop under the tyrannical rule of Sarah.

"Hey, Nina, quit lazing around there." The same tyrant scowled at her from across the kitchen. "Make yourself useful. There're some tables in the bar area that need clearing."

Sarah would make a perfect sergeant major, Nina thought as she left the kitchen. The bar was crowded, too, but despite that, Vince came over while she was loading her bus pan.

"You look wiped out," he said sympathetically.

Nina was about to agree but held her tongue. She didn't want Joe hearing from his bartender as well as his chef how inadequate she was. Squaring her shoulders, she lifted the dirty plates more energetically.

"I'm managing." She dropped the plates into the bus pan. "So where's Joe tonight?" She thought he'd be around, if only to intervene in case she was a complete disaster, but she hadn't seen him all evening, and that had made her first shift more tiring. If Joe had been there, she'd have made darn sure to not show any hint of exhaustion.

"Thursday night is soccer practice. Joe's the team captain, so he never misses a session."

It figured that Joe played soccer. Those long legs and athletic build of his were made for the game. And she wasn't surprised he was the captain of his team. From what she'd seen, Joe liked directing the action, being in charge. She wondered what he looked like after playing soccer. He'd be all muddy and sweaty, and he'd have to strip off and take a shower... She gave herself a mental slap. Damn, she shouldn't be fantasizing about her new boss in the shower.

She grabbed her bottle of ammonia and sprayed the cleared table fiercely before attacking it with her cloth.

"You're enthusiastic." Vince said. "When your shift's over, why don't you stop by for a drink? It should be a lot quieter by then."

"Thanks, I'd like that."

Vince was a nice guy. It would be a pleasant change to chat with him instead of Sarah or Joe. But an hour later, when Sarah finally allowed her to go, all Nina could think about was falling into bed. Her entire body ached, and if she sat down at the bar she was sure she'd collapse headfirst into her drink. After struggling all night to keep up the pretense that she was an experienced worker, she couldn't let people see her fall to pieces.

And that went for Joe, especially. When she returned to the bar and saw him at the counter talking with Vince, she pinned back her aching shoulders and forced a spring to her step, ignoring her screaming arches. No way would she let him see how wiped out she was.

"How did your first shift go?" Joe gave her a thorough once-over. Those dark brown eyes didn't seem to miss a thing.

Standing tall, despite the spasm in her lower back, she smoothed away her hair. "I didn't injure anyone, and I only broke a couple of plates, if that's what you mean."

He grinned, the corners of his eyes crinkling up. Next to Joe's spruced-up freshness, she felt even more frazzled. He'd showered, judging by the dampness of his hair, which gleamed like polished ebony. A lustrous lock curled across his forehead. His tanned skin glowed after his exercise, and his jaw was freshly shaven. Her stomach did a weird little flip. Joe looked fantastic and incredibly sexy. A sudden, inconvenient urge to stroke his jaw and smooth back that stray lock of hair ambushed her.

"Great." He tilted his chin at her boots. "So your feet aren't killing you?"

"Not at all." She stuck out one foot and wriggled it around. "I could go clubbing right now."

"No clubs around here, but we do have alcohol." He gestured at the bar stool next to him. "Want a drink?"

Oh, boy, did she need a drink. And a seat. But if she sank

into that stool, she'd never get up. Worse, she wouldn't be able to stop ogling or sniffing him. Bad idea.

"I'll pass." She shook her head. "Think I'll just take a shower and go to bed."

"Good idea. We're expecting a full house tomorrow and there's a heap of cleaning still to be done. Can you start at seven thirty? Guests sometimes arrive before noon, and I like their rooms to be ready."

Nina's feet throbbed in protest. "Seven thirty? No problem. I'll set my alarm."

Joe studied her for a few moments, as if he knew that every muscle in her body was crying out for relief. He leaned a little closer. Vince had gone to the other end of the bar, leaving them temporarily isolated.

"Sure you're coping?" Joe lowered his voice. "You look wrecked."

For a second she was almost taken in by his sympathy before she wondered if this was a trap. If she admitted her total exhaustion, Joe might use it as an excuse to get rid of her.

"Thank you for your concern," she said smoothly, "but I'm fine. I'll see you in the morning. Good night." She turned to go without waiting for his reply.

"Night, Nina," he said after her. "Have a good rest; you'll be busy tomorrow."

The warning note in his tone made her stiffen her aching back as she walked away. Joe Farina would not get the better of her.

Later, it wasn't Joe but the shower that got the better of her. She'd returned to her dreary room, stripped off her clothes, wrapped herself in a bath towel, and walked down the long, drafty passage to the bathroom. There, under a harsh fluorescent light that made the white-tiled bathroom feel like a mortuary, she'd turned on the faucet, desperately looking forward to a hot shower to ease the kinks from her weary muscles.

The pipes creaked as tepid water dribbled down her back. Impatient, she twisted the hot water tap another inch. The lukewarm trickle persisted. She spun the tap some more and *scalding*-hot water jetted over her, making her squeal. Joe hadn't been kidding when he warned her this bathroom wasn't renovated. She battled with the faucet some more until she had the temperature just right.

She'd just massaged shampoo into her hair and the ache in her back was beginning to ease when, without warning, the hot water cut out. One moment she was warm and relaxed, the next she was attacked by stinging cold water. Startled, she frantically twisted the tap, but freezing water continued to hammer her. Swearing a blue streak, she managed to turn off the water and staggered out of the shower.

Shampoo stung her eyes, she was wet and chilly, and her muscles were once again tied up in knots. She wrapped her towel around her shivering body and sank down on the toilet seat. Her body shook, her chin trembled, and a sob hiccuped out of her. Followed by another, and another, and suddenly she couldn't stop the sobs bubbling out.

Last night she'd slept at her dad's golf resort in an executive suite complete with spa bath and an open fireplace. Now she was shivering in a nightmare bathroom with no hot water and only a dreary bedroom and another day of hard labor ahead of her. Why on earth was she doing this? What was she trying to prove to herself…or to Joe? It didn't matter if he thought she wasn't up to the job. She'd only met him today; she didn't need his approval.

This whole "going incognito" stunt was insane and point-less, and she was suffering for no good reason. How stupid could she be? She pushed to her feet, exasperated at her own lunacy, and marched out of the bathroom. Her damp feet slapped on the floor as she tramped down the hall. Just as she reached her bedroom, the door to Joe's office opened, and Joe stepped out. Instantly her rib cage constricted. She'd assumed this part of the inn was deserted.

He scrutinized her, his face expressionless. "Trouble with the shower?"

She huffed at the wet, soapy strands of hair hanging over her eyes. "You didn't tell me the inn was haunted. That shower back there is possessed! First it scalded me, and then it tried to drown me in ice water."

The corners of his lips twitched. "That shower's only used by employees, and not very often. You just need to jiggle the faucets."

"No, I'm not jiggling anything because that's it. I've had it."

His eyebrows shot up. "You're quitting already? I thought you'd at least make it through twenty-four hours. What happened to all that turning-over-a-new-leaf shit you were sprouting earlier?"

The edge in his voice made her bristle. "Don't judge me until you've walked a mile in my shoes, buddy. You don't know what I've been through today."

It had been a day from hell. She'd discovered no one ap-preciated her hard work or thought her capable of anything, and then she'd crashed her car, hatched a stupid, *stupid* scheme to prove herself, met a man hot enough to melt her bones, worked her ass off, and now she was wet, shivering, and half naked in front of that same hot, infuriating man.

Joe's shoulders stiffened. "Oh, yeah? Well, let me tell you about *my* day. I waited hours for you to turn up, and when you finally did, you clearly showed you had no experience. But I let you stay, despite my better judgment and knowing Sarah didn't approve, and this is how you repay me. By throwing it in my face."

"Hey, I haven't thrown anything at anyone. I've cleaned your bathrooms, cleared your tables, washed your dishes, let Sarah boss me around. God knows why!"

"For someone with no experience, you sure are picky. You should be grateful for the opportunities you've been given." He exhaled a long breath, as if struggling to hold on to his temper, and held up both hands, palms facing out. "But don't let me stop you. Frankly, I'm not surprised."

"What's that supposed to mean?"

"I mean I knew from the start you didn't have it in you."

She pulled the towel tighter around her chest. Joe's criticism hurt more than it should. He was a stranger, and she shouldn't care what he thought of her. But, perversely, she did. His words were an echo of the conversation she'd eavesdropped on between her so-called friends. *They* didn't think she had it in her to succeed on her own, and Joe shared the same view. And since he didn't know her true identity, that made it even worse.

"If you thought that, why did you take me on in the first place?"

"I dunno. Call me crazy."

Joe's gaze wandered over her, lingering on her bare

skin. His mocha eyes softened slightly, and a flush of warmth feathered through her. Why this man had such an effect on her, she didn't know, but she couldn't seem to control her reactions. A second ago he'd been telling her off, criticizing her, but suddenly the mood had shifted, and there was something wistful, almost seductive in his sweeping scan. But then he shook his head, and that seemed to break the spell.

"You're welcome to stay the night," he said, all business-like. "There's an early morning bus service to Fort Bragg to-morrow. You might pick up a coffee shop job there." He dug into the pocket of his jeans and drew out his wallet. "And I'll pay you for the shift you've just worked."

Nina recoiled from the money he offered her. "No, thank you. You're giving me a bed for the night, and I had a meal in the bar and I broke two plates. I'm sure that makes us even."

She wasn't going to accept charity from anyone, especially not Joe. She might only have a few dollars on her, but she still had her cell phone. Tomorrow morning she'd call her dad. He'd organize help, probably send the company helicopter to pick her up. And then she'd arrange for her BMW to be hauled out of the quarry and transported to San Francisco. Her heart sank lower at the prospect of telling her dad what had happened, but it seemed the only sensible thing to do.

Joe gave her an enigmatic look before pocketing the money. "Have it your way." He paused, then shrugged. "I might not see you in the morning, so good luck and stay out of trouble, Nina."

Not waiting for a response, he turned and strode away like he'd just completed a distasteful chore.

Chapter Three

Joe spent a restless night, plagued by thoughts of Nina. He barely knew the woman, but she intrigued him and bothered him equally. His instincts had warned him she wasn't suitable for the job, that she was bound to cause trouble, and trouble was the last thing he needed in his busy life. But then he'd damn well let her stay, because his common sense had been overruled by other instincts. Base instincts he tried to ignore but couldn't.

As he tossed under the sheets, he couldn't help remembering Nina standing in front of him, naked except for a bath towel. Even as they argued, his senses had been invaded by her moist, sudsy skin and her blue eyes glaring at him through her slick hair. A caveman urge had boiled in him to yank her into his arms and find out with his lips and fingers exactly how silky her skin was.

She hadn't seemed to care that only a thin scrap of fabric stood between him and her lithe body. She'd taunted him, letting the towel slip an inch or two, revealing the tops of her breasts, and he'd fought the compulsion to silence her by bringing his mouth down on hers, hard and hot and demanding. Nina got his motor running in overdrive, but he didn't care for it.

After Deanne, he'd vowed never to lose his head over a woman again, and for four whole years he'd kept that promise without breaking a sweat. Until Nina arrived and jolted something alive in him, something that threatened his vow. Fortunately, he wouldn't have his resolve tested any further, because she was leaving as suddenly as she'd arrived. Thank God. But he didn't feel as relieved as he should be.

The sun was barely up by the time he'd finished his morning run and showered, changed, and breakfasted. He had a busy day ahead. First, he had a meeting with the nurse manager at the nursing home a twenty-minute drive away where his nonna Lina now lived since her car accident. He never missed the monthly meetings. As far as he could tell, his grandmother was content enough at the home, but he liked to be aware of any changes to her routine.

Then it was back to Hartley for a committee meeting at ten, which would take at least an hour, so by the time he got back to the Comet Inn, Nina would be gone. He wouldn't have to see her and become further aggravated. Or stimulated.

Just before eleven, he walked into the inn and made straight for his office. Now that Nina had left, he'd have to scramble to find a replacement, plus there was all the cleaning she was supposed to do—work he'd probably end up doing himself.

He was at his desk searching for the number of the

employment agency when he heard a clattering noise down the hall followed by a muffled curse. Poking his head out of his office door, he spotted Nina battling with the industrial vacuum cleaner. The two coffees he'd drunk suddenly began burning a hole in his stomach.

He walked out and stood in front of her. "What are you doing?"

She dumped the vacuum cleaner on the floor, wiped the back of her forearm across her brow, and blinked at him. "Doing weights with oversize vacuum cleaners is a hobby of mine, didn't you know?"

Her face was hot and flushed, and strands of her blonde hair stuck to her temples. She wore the same clothes as yesterday, the T-shirt more wrinkled, the leg of her jeans stained. She looked sweaty and grubby and scrappy. Something in his chest flipped over and squeezed the air from his lungs.

"You've decided to stay?" He should have been annoyed, but instead couldn't help the corners of his mouth tweaking up.

"Looks like it," she said.

"Because you want to prove yourself to me?"

"I'm doing this for me. Nothing to do with you."

"Nothing at all? Not even a tiny bit?" Joe leaned his shoulder against the wall. He shouldn't be feeling this lighthearted just because she'd decided to stay.

"Okay, you got me. Yeah, I admit it. I'm staying because I have a massive crush on you." She swept her blue gaze over him, assessing him, and a strange tingling raced across Joe's chest. Even his damn nipples were reacting to her.

He managed not to swallow. "You do?"

"Sure. I mean, no girl could resist all that Italian

stallionness oozing out of you." She fluttered a hand at him. "So you'd better be ready to catch me in case I swoon at your feet."

He hid his amusement. "And you're just assuming I'd be happy to let you stay on?"

The sass slipped from her expression, and her mouth fell open. *Aha, she hadn't thought of that one.*

"Don't you want me to?"

"Well, let's see now." He made a show of stroking his chin and pretending to ponder the matter. "Do I want someone who's inexperienced and has a conniption when the shower acts up?"

Nina's cheeks grew pinker. "I had a bad day yesterday. The shower was the straw that broke this camel's back."

"And I can guarantee you'll have another bad day in the future, probably not far off. Are you going to threaten to pack up again? Because I don't have the time or inclination to be your personal cheer squad every time you chip a fingernail or something."

She swallowed, looking like she was battling to hold her tongue. "I hate to break it to you, but being a personal cheer squad is not your forte."

Joe couldn't help grinning at that. "True. I don't go in for that managerial motivational-speak."

"If I promise to hunker down, can I keep the job?"

She flashed him a winning smile that sent a powerful shaft of lust straight to his crotch. *Hoh, boy.* How was he going to maintain the hard-ass boss attitude if one smile from her could give him a semi-on? He never got involved with his staff; that was a hard and fast rule. Apart from it being unprofessional, a messy entanglement could sour the tight-knit team he'd built up and, even worse, a lawsuit could ruin him, especially now, when his finances were stretched tight and he was struggling to get a bank loan.

He cleared his throat. "Uh, well, let's say you're on probation for the next month." He scratched his head, waiting for his blood to return northward to his brain. "What have you done so far this morning?"

Nina expelled a breath. "I've changed the linen in the rooms where the guests checked out and cleaned the bathrooms. Now I'm about to do the carpets."

His eyebrows shot up. "You did all that on your own initiative?"

"It's not that hard to figure out." She hefted up the vacuum cleaner. "Now, if you'll excuse me, I have more cleaning to do."

"Let me carry that for you." He reached for the vacuum, but she shook her head.

"You don't usually do that for your maids, do you?"

"No, but…" It didn't seem right to let her lug that bulky piece of equipment up the stairs. Not when he was imagining himself kissing her.

"I can manage." To prove her words, she shuffled past him and headed for the reception lobby.

Joe watched her progress. As she reached the foot of the staircase, Vince rushed out of the bar and swooped the vacuum cleaner out of her hands before she could say anything.

"Let me give you a hand," Vince chirped.

Joe waited for Nina to tell Vince she didn't need his help, but instead she gave him a brilliant beam and bounced after him. Joe scowled and turned back to his office.

An hour later, Joe was outside the inn pinning up a poster for the upcoming Hartley Food and Wine Festival when Vince ambled up to him.

"So you never told me how the bank meeting went yesterday," Vince said.

"Not good. The loan officer didn't like my numbers, so my application was rejected."

Vince grimaced. "That sucks."

"Yeah." Joe shook his head. Nina's arrival had temporarily distracted him, but now he had to face his financial difficulties. The Comet Inn was doing well, but Joe wanted to expand into the high-end B&B market. Six months ago he'd bought a grand but dilapidated mansion on a fifty-acre block just out of town. Since it was an estate sale, he'd purchased it before securing funding for the renovations. The property had great business potential, but so far he'd had no luck finding a bank willing to loan him the sizable amount he needed.

"What will you do?" Vince pulled on his lower lip, looking worried. "You're not going to give in to those Beaumont pricks, are you?"

Joe's back tensed. "No way. I'd sooner pull out my fingernails than let Carson Beaumont take my property."

He'd never met Carson Beaumont. Instead, the multi-millionaire jerk had sent his black-suited corporate thugs to cajole and threaten Joe into selling his proposed B&B to them. Not that Beaumont, Inc. was interested in running a B&B. No, they were interested in the ocean views and the road access his property would give them to their potential new development. They were interested in razing the grand old mansion to the ground and plunking down a flashy megaresort that would totally ruin Hartley.

"I'm not done yet," Joe said. "There are other banks."

But he wasn't filled with hope. The loan officer had been fidgety, embarrassed even when he rejected Joe's application. As if there was more to it than he was letting on. Joe was beginning to suspect Beaumont, Inc. was somehow behind his difficulties in getting a bank loan.

"Good." Vince nodded. "I'd hate to see a Beaumont resort here. They've already spoiled Sonoma. Why can't they stay the hell out of Hartley?"

"I'm working on it, Vince."

Vince returned to the inn while Joe finished pinning the poster. He walked back into the reception lobby just as Nina appeared.

"Hi," she said. "Got a minute?"

"Yeah," he replied, his interest piqued by her furtive manner.

She plucked at her jeans, looking slightly embarrassed. "The thing is, I had all my clothes stolen, remember? This is all I own at the moment. I can wash my T-shirt and underwear each night, but if I don't get some spare things soon, I'm going to start smelling funky. And I really need to get some more comfortable shoes, because these boots are killing me. I know it's a bit much to ask, but could I have an advance on my wages? Say, forty dollars?"

"Sure." He reached into his back pocket for his wallet and pulled out a couple of twenties.

"Thanks." Her cheeks were pink as she took the money from him. "I'd better put this in my room." She hurried away from him, hands in the pockets of her jeans.

"I saw that!" Sarah stood in the entrance to the bar, her arms crossed and a black scowl darkening her forehead. "It's bad enough you hiring her on a whim, but now you're giving her money, too?"

"Not giving, lending."

"There's no way she's ever worked in a coffee shop. After what I saw last night, I doubt she has any service experience at all." Sarah was getting even more worked up. "There's something fishy about her. I'm convinced she's hiding something."

Maybe Sarah had a point, Joe mused. Nina had seemed cagey about her past. But then again, plenty of people were. She wasn't the first to come here looking for a fresh start.

Joe shrugged. "Even if she is, it doesn't mean she's not honest."

"Are you into her? Is that why she's got you twisted around her little finger?"

Joe's jaw clamped tight. "I think you're forgetting who's in charge of this place."

He'd spoken evenly, but it was enough for Sarah to blush, a rare occurrence for her. "If I stepped out of line, I'm sorry," she said, "but maybe you're forgetting I'm more than just your chef. I'm your friend, too, and I'd hate to see you being taken for a ride."

Joe sighed. Sarah was right; they *were* friends, and she had every right to call him out on his peculiar behavior. But it irked him that she thought Nina had some kind of hold over him. She didn't. Sure, he had a hard time not thinking about her, and every conversation they had set off tiny fireworks in him, but he wasn't *enslaved* by her. He wasn't going to let a little inconvenient lust fog up his brain.

"D'you really think a girl like Nina could have me twisted around her little finger?" he scoffed.

Sarah slowly shook her head. "Guess not. You get plenty of women throwing themselves at you, and you never lose your head over any of them."

"Damn right I don't." Deanne had taught him his lesson. Since then, he made sure his amorous adventures were strictly temporary. That way his emotions were never in danger. Besides, he didn't have the time or energy for a serious relationship. He had the Comet Inn, his grandmother, and his new business venture, as well as his commitments to the Hartley business community and his soccer team, all keeping him busy. A serious girlfriend would only complicate his already overloaded life.

"Fine. You can handle it." Sarah turned to head back to the kitchen and said over her shoulder, "Besides, that Nina Summers hardly seems like your type."

Joe was left standing there, his teeth grinding. How did Sarah know what his type was? Did he even have a type? Judging by the way his body reacted to Nina's presence since she'd arrived, he had to admit not only was she his type, but she was also in a unique class of her own made specifically to tempt him.

Rubbing his face, Joe headed for his office. He needed some time alone.

• • •

Friday passed in a blur of drudgery. Nina wasn't a stranger to hard work, but by the end of the day she realized that weekly Zumba and yoga sessions were no preparation for being a maid or busgirl.

Joe ran a tight ship at the Comet Inn, and everyone was expected to pull his or her weight. Though he was the undisputed boss of the place, he pitched in wherever he was needed, worked harder than anyone else, and his employees seemed to genuinely like and respect him.

Nina didn't get any special concessions from him because she was new and inexperienced. After she'd readied the rooms for their Friday night guests, he inspected her work and found several things she'd missed or hadn't done to his satisfaction. As he spelled out her shortcomings, he wore a slightly cynical expression, as if he expected her to argue, but she didn't. Determined not to give him the chance to criticize her attitude, she smiled blandly and got on with the job.

Friday night at the Comet Inn was frenetic, and even though Joe hired extra staff for his busy nights, they were still swamped. By the time the kitchen closed, Nina was staggering on her feet, so fatigued that Sarah's whiplash tongue barely penetrated the fog of exhaustion enveloping her. She tossed her soiled apron into the laundry bin and trudged past the bar. She'd meant to hang out with Vince, but she was too tired to socialize, and besides, Vince seemed busy.

In the lobby she bumped into Joe, and, with her last ounce of energy, she mustered up a nod for him.

"Good night. I'm not even attempting that freaky shower tonight. I'm going to fall straight into bed." She was too exhausted to even keep up the pretense of coping in front of Joe.

His dark eyes softened as he reached out and clasped

her shoulder. "Didn't you have any breaks today?"

The weight of his hand sent a warm buzz through her. "Not really. It took longer than I expected to get the last guest rooms in order."

"You're entitled to a thirty-minute break every five hours. You should've taken them." His thumb rotated absentmindedly on her shoulder at the neckline of her T-shirt, and the feel of his thumb pad against her skin emitted a rush of heat through her body. Her fatigue vanished, replaced by a startling, troublesome desire.

"I want to pass probation."

"But I don't want you passing out," Joe said, his eyes heavy lidded, enigmatic. "It's too bad the inn is booked solid or you could've used one of the free bathrooms." He paused, then added casually, "You can always take a shower at my place."

With you? The question burst into her mind, accompanied by graphic images of showering with Joe. Hard muscle, cascading water, Joe's firm ass clasped in her hands, and his hungry lips moving over hers… Sexual need spiked in her, sharpening to a tight, hot throb between her legs. Holy hell. She had a full-on lust for this guy.

"Your p-place?" she stuttered, her lungs not working. "Uh, where's that?"

"About ten minutes out of town. I've got a house on a few acres. Nice and quiet."

She cleared her throat, which had suddenly become the Sahara Desert. "The others would get suspicious if the maid took a shower at your place." She could feel her face growing red.

He huffed out a breath, looking almost regretful. "Yeah,

they probably would."

She should've grabbed his offer as soon as he'd made it. But that would've been reckless. "I don't want people to think I'm any different from the last maid you had."

His eyes crinkled at the corners. "The last maid was a bodybuilder who could whip this place into shape in a few hours without breaking a sweat. I doubt you could be any more different from her, but I get your point." His hand dropped away, and Nina missed the contact, but at least she could breathe again.

Now that Joe wasn't touching her, common sense returned. She hadn't gone to all this trouble disguising her identity just to hook up with a hunky Italian who offered her free hot showers in his private home. Besides, Joe's offer might be perfectly innocent. He might only be a concerned employer. He might not be attracted to her at all, because how attractive could she be in these icky clothes that she'd worn for two straight days? Suddenly self-conscious of her grimy appearance, she ran her fingers through her messy hair and tugged at her stained T-shirt.

"Are there any shops open tomorrow where I could get some cheap clothing? I really need to get out of these."

She caught a sudden spark in his eyes, as if the idea of her getting out of clothes intrigued him. "Try the thrift store down the road."

"Okay."

"What size are you?" His gaze traveled lazily over her breasts and hips.

Nina concentrated on her breathing. "Why?"

"My sister, Carla, keeps clothes at my place. I could give you some of hers."

"Wouldn't she mind?"

"I doubt it. She took most of her stuff when she moved to New York a few months ago. Anything precious left behind she packed in boxes marked 'Do not touch.'"

"Oh. Is she your only sibling?" Nina asked, curiosity overcoming her.

"Yup. Our parents died more than a decade ago, so we're close."

"I'm sorry about your parents. I lost my mom when I was thirteen." She paused for a breath. "So what's your sister doing in New York? College?"

"She graduated from Princeton this year. Now she's taken an internship at the UN." Pride animated his voice.

"Wow. She sounds like a go-getter."

"That she is. She wanted to do the internship before entering grad school. She's only twenty-two, but she's always been interested in public policy. I wouldn't be surprised if she ends up becoming the secretary-general one day."

Carla Farina was younger than Nina, but it sounded like she'd had her act together for ages. Which made Nina feel like even more of an underachiever.

"Carla won't mind if I give you a few of her things," Joe continued, surveying her legs. "She's a little taller than you, but just as thin."

Joe had given her a job and a place to stay and loaned her money. If she started accepting clothes from him, she'd be in danger of becoming a complete charity case, and that wasn't why she'd embarked on this lifestyle change.

"That's very generous of you, but I can't," she said. "You've already done more than enough for me, but thanks for the offer."

"Sure." Joe lifted his shoulders. "Let me know if you change your mind."

Wishing him good night, she inched past him.

When she'd hatched this crazy scheme, she hadn't factored in the possibility of men, and even if she had, nothing in her past experience could have prepared her for the fizzing pull of attraction she felt every time Joe came near her, an attraction she couldn't seem to suppress or control. She hadn't felt that way since, well, forever. Even Oliver, her rat ex, whom she'd supposedly fallen madly in love with, had never affected her the way Joe did.

Which meant staying here in Hartley could do more harm than good to her emotional well-being. If she had any sense, she'd cut her losses and leave. But she knew she wouldn't, and it wasn't just because she was reckless and stubborn and the prospect of slinking back to her old life— a life she had to return to in three weeks' time—left a bad taste in her mouth. Quitting now wasn't an option. But neither was giving in to her pesky weakness for Joe.

• • •

The thrift shop smelled of musty books and old clothes, but Nina didn't mind. She had Saturday afternoon off, and it was a relief to take a break and browse through the store. She'd already visited the general store and bought underwear and toiletries. Now she needed some fresh clothing and comfortable shoes.

After riffling through the racks, she had an armful of secondhand gear to try on. The friendly middle-aged lady in charge of the store directed her to a tiny cubicle screened off by a flimsy curtain. She had just struggled into black denim jeans and a snug-fitting, lemon-colored sweater when she heard the distinctive timbre of Joe's voice greeting the store clerk.

"Morning, Mrs. Stewart. Just dropping off some extra linen from the inn." There was the sound of a heavy bag landing on the counter.

"Oh, isn't that sweet of you," Mrs. Stewart said. "And how are you, Joe? How's your grandmother and business at the inn?"

For a while the two chatted warmly. Nina had frozen the instant she recognized Joe's voice. She'd hoped to remain in the changing cubicle until he left, but the way he and the shop clerk were chatting, she'd be stuck in here till Christmas. Oh, well, then, she'd just have to go out and face him, because there was no mirror in the cubicle. Drawing in her stomach muscles, she pushed the curtain aside and stepped out.

Both Joe and Mrs. Stewart turned to look at her, but it was Joe's reaction that Nina sought out. He eyeballed the black denim that hugged her thighs and the lemon sweater that clung to her breasts. She wasn't exactly well endowed in the bosom department, but the stretchy fabric and Joe's keen inspection made her feel several cup sizes bigger. And more self-conscious, too. Which was weird. And weirdly exciting.

"Found some bargains?" Joe nodded at Mrs. Stewart. "Nina is my new maid at the inn. She was looking for some clothing, so I directed her here."

Mrs. Stewart studied Nina with fresh interest. "You're not a Hartley girl, are you, dear?"

Nina smiled. "No. I'm from San Francisco."

"I see. It's a permanent move, then?" Mrs. Stewart asked.

"I don't think Nina's made that decision yet," Joe said. "Besides, she's still on probation at the inn."

"You're lucky to have a job there," the store clerk said to Nina. "Joe's a good boss, and he's an important fella in this town."

Intrigued, Nina moved forward and rested her hip against the counter. "So Joe's the big cheese around Hartley, is he?"

"That he is. We're very lucky to have him."

Nina sneaked a peek at Joe. Mrs. Stewart's lavish praise made him look a little sheepish. Sheepish and cute. *Aw, how adorable…* She blinked in surprise at her thoughts. Adorable? Joe? How could that be?

"I suppose he'll be running for mayor one of these days." Nina decided to tease him.

Mrs. Stewart nodded, all solemn. "He'll get my vote, that's for sure."

"I have no ambitions to run for mayor," Joe cut in. "I don't have the time, for one thing. Not when I have snarky new maids to supervise."

Mrs. Stewart nudged him with her elbow. "Don't tease the poor girl, she's just started."

"That's okay, Mrs. Stewart." Nina waved a nonchalant hand at Joe. "I know I've been giving him some attitude."

His lips curved upward. "I can handle your attitude, sweet pea, as long as you get the job done."

The "sweet pea" coupled with the grin he flashed her made her gulp. That lazy, sensuous smile of his was lethal. With Joe only a few feet away from her, there didn't seem to be enough oxygen in the overcrowded little store.

Determined not to let him see how much he affected

her, she flicked her fingers through her hair. "That's good to know, because I've got plenty of attitude to spare."

He laughed, a warm, indulgent chuckle. "Never a dull moment with you, is there, Nina?" Turning back to the shop clerk, he patted the counter. "Thanks, Mrs. Stewart, I'll see you around." As he made for the door, he nodded to Nina. "I like that yellow sweater. Highlights the snark in you."

Nina couldn't help staring after him as he exited the store. She continued to peer out the window as he got into his pickup truck and drove off.

Behind her, Mrs. Stewart made a little humming noise. "He's a nice boy, that Joe Farina. And so hardworking. I don't know how he manages."

Nina played with a bowl of bracelets sitting on the counter. "Yes, he works long hours at the inn."

"It's not just the Comet Inn. He has his grandmother to look after. Oh, his uncle and aunt visit, but they have the farm to run, so poor Joe has the lion's share of responsibility."

"I knew about his sister, Carla, but not about his grandmother." She shouldn't be so interested in Joe's personal life, but everything about him fascinated her, and clearly Mrs. Stewart had no qualms talking about her favorite Hartley citizen.

"She helped Joe raise his sister after their parents died. But about four years ago, just after Joe bought the Comet Inn, his grandmother had a bad car accident. Left her with long-term disabilities. Oh, she's mobile enough, but she needs twenty-four-hour care, which is why she's in a nursing home now. I volunteer there, too. Joe visits his grandma like clockwork."

"Sounds like he has plenty of responsibilities."

"He's also on the business council, and this year he's helping to organize the Food and Wine Festival, as if he doesn't have enough to do."

Nina nodded. Busy, busy, busy. That seemed to be Joe's modus operandi.

"How old is he?" she asked, trying to sound casual.

"He turned thirty in July. His sister threw him a birthday party before she left."

"That's Carla, right? The one who's interning at the UN?"

"That's her." Mrs. Stewart gave Nina a mischievous smile. "You seem mighty interested in Joe."

Nina affected a nonchalant shrug. "Yeah, well. He sounds like a regular hero around here."

She had to admit she was impressed. Joe was only five years her senior, and yet he already owned a thriving business. On top of that he had an ailing grandmother in what must be an expensive facility and had raised his younger sister after losing their parents. He'd achieved all this off his own sweat. Joe was a self-motivated, self-made success—the complete opposite of her—and that made her feel inadequate, if she were honest.

She bit her lip. Feeling inadequate didn't lessen her attraction to him, though.

Mrs. Stewart clucked as she tidied a stack of flyers for the Hartley Food and Wine Festival on her counter. "One day that Joe Farina is going to make some lucky girl very happy, but it's not going to happen anytime soon, I'm afraid."

Nina pressed her lips together. She was *not* going to ask. She wasn't…but it was too tempting. "Why's that?" she blurted.

"Girls are always throwing themselves at him, but he rarely goes out with one for very long." Shaking her head, Mrs. Stewart added darkly, "I blame it on his last steady girlfriend. They broke up not long after his grandmother's car accident... That Deanne has a lot to answer for."

Nina chewed on her lip as curiosity burned inside her. What had this Deanne woman done to make Joe gun-shy of relationships? Had he been head over heels in love with her? Had she broken his heart?

Nina put a clamp on her shameful inquisitiveness. She shouldn't speculate about Joe's love life. It was none of her business, and she was already too enthralled by him. He was just her boss, and that was the way it would stay.

"I'd better try on the rest of those clothes," she said, heading for the changing cubicle.

She picked out a few more items and decided to wear the black jeans and lemon sweater instead of changing back into her dirty clothes. Next, she moved onto the rack of secondhand shoes but was appalled to find that the only comfortable shoes in her size were a pair of hideous turquoise Crocs. She winced at her dorky reflection in the mirror while Mrs. Stewart hid a smile.

"So practical for working at the inn," Mrs. Stewart said. "Will you be taking them?"

Her ego said no, but her toes said yes, and for now her toes won. Nina sighed and nodded. "I'll wear them. My boots are killing me."

While Mrs. Stewart rang up her purchases, a couple of well-dressed, middle-aged ladies entered the shop. Judging by their country club outfits they were clearly donors, not customers. They placed their bulging shopping bags on the counter and peered at Nina with expectant curiosity.

Mrs. Stewart lost no time in providing them with details. "This is Nina. She's Joe's new maid at the Comet Inn."

The ladies murmured greetings and studied Nina with keen interest.

"Just moved into town, then?" one of them asked, and Nina nodded.

"A permanent move, is it?" the other asked.

Boy, how inquisitive these people were. Making a non-committal reply, Nina backed away. Was it just Hartley, or were all country towns so into other people's business?

"Oh, my." One of the ladies stared at Nina's Crocs. "How…er, colorful."

Her friend nudged her. "Come on, Babs. She can't help it. This is why we donate our old things."

A hot flush engulfed Nina's face. Like these well-to-do women, she'd donated a lot of her belongings to thrift stores, but now she knew what it was like receiving charity out of necessity, and she'd never felt more humbled.

Nina made a polite excuse and quickly exited the store, feeling everyone's eyes fixed on her. Outside, she sucked in a deep breath and tried to shake off the sensation of suffocation that had come over her. The women in the store, including Mrs. Stewart, were friendly enough, but they took an awful lot of interest in other people's business.

What if someone here in Hartley discovered who she really was? Her dad wasn't exactly a secret millionaire, or a discreet one. Over the years he'd ruffled a few feathers, caused a stir with some of his more controversial developments. Like his mega golf course resort in nearby Sonoma County.

When she'd been there a few days ago, she'd learned how the resort almost hadn't happened. The locals had campaigned vigorously against the proposed development a few years back, and some of the protests had gotten quite nasty. Carson Beaumont hadn't been afraid to show up at some of the heated town meetings and speak his mind. He'd made some minor concessions, but the resort had been built, despite the strong opposition. Even now resentment still lingered in the community, and these small country towns had long memories. If people found out she was Carson Beaumont's daughter, she'd be about as welcome as an outbreak of lice.

She walked farther down the block. Around her, people strolled along the sidewalks, and most stores were open. It was midday Saturday. This might be Hartley's busiest day of the week, but to her it suddenly struck her as empty, isolated, and a long, long way from everything she was used to. She'd never consciously labeled herself a city girl, but now she had a sudden biting need for crowds, traffic, and noise.

She glanced over her shoulder at the thrift store she'd just left. The store clerk and the country club ladies were still squinting at her through the window. What were they saying about her? She'd thought she could forget who she was in this small country town, but now tongues were clacking. People might not know her true identity, but they were still talking about her, and it made her uncomfortable. Maybe it had been a mistake to think she could reinvent herself here.

She walked to the end of the street, where the beach stretched out, and sat on a bench. As the wind whipped her hair around her cheeks, a sense of loss and loneliness welled up inside her.

Who was she kidding, hiding out in Hartley? She couldn't escape being a Beaumont. She couldn't suddenly change her identity on a whim. She couldn't be someone else just by wearing secondhand clothes and pretending to be a maid.

And Joe only made things worse. She couldn't think straight around him when her body reacted so strongly to his presence. The more time she spent with him, the more she'd succumb to his charms, but having an affair with him was out of the question. He didn't know who she was, and he was so different from her, so embedded in the fabric of this sleepy little coastal village. She didn't belong here, and she shouldn't be hanging around Joe any longer.

She leaped to her feet and hurried back up the main street. In five minutes she reached the Comet Inn. Feeling like a thief, she dashed inside and scurried past the lobby, hoping to catch Joe alone in his office. But his office was empty. Disappointed, she sagged against the doorjamb.

"What's up, sweet pea?" Joe said from behind her.

She whirled around, her heart jerking. That was the second time today he'd called her sweet pea. As Joe advanced, her libido surged in a sudden, violent flood, and she couldn't drag her gaze away from him—didn't want to, either.

Joe. Shirtless. Showing off a sleeveless white undershirt that clung to the strongly defined muscles of his chest. A few streaks of grease were smeared on his undershirt and face. His right biceps gleamed as he gripped a heavy-looking wrench. His flash of white teeth got her pulses fluttering.

"I've fixed the faucets in the bathroom. You'll be able to have all the hot showers you want now."

"Th-thanks." Oh, God, why did he have to go and do a nice thing like that for her? And why did he have to look so hot and hunky and stripped-down gorgeous? As he lifted an arm to wipe his cheek, the muscles in his shoulder rippled and her heartbeat stammered.

He transferred the wrench from one hand to the other, slowly looking her over. "Glad you took my advice on the clothes."

Her body tingled where his gaze lingered as if he'd touched her. He shouldn't be looking at her like that. He shouldn't be having this effect on her, damn it.

"I didn't have much choice at the thrift store." She lifted one foot to show him the Crocs. "As you can see."

His lips twitched. "You still look good." His expression grew a little more sober, as if he sensed something was off kilter. "What did you want to see me about?"

Joe thinks I look good. Not the most lavish compliment she'd ever received, but it threw her so completely that for a moment she forgot what she'd rushed inside to tell him. Then it came back to her—she was quitting, leaving Joe, the job, and Hartley after all.

She swallowed, conscious now of the seriousness of what she was about to do. Joe hadn't thought much of her in the beginning, but over the past two days she'd sensed his opinion changing. So much so he'd even fixed the shower for her. That meant he wanted her to stay, didn't it? If she resigned now, he'd be annoyed, scornful. He'd accuse her of wasting his time again, of being fickle and unreliable. It shouldn't matter, because once she left she'd never see him again, but deep down it did. Despite her reasoning, Joe's opinion mattered to her.

"I, er..." She hunted for something—anything—to say. "I went for a walk down to the beach. It's, uh, pretty around here."

"Glad you noticed." His eyes narrowed. "Is that what you came rushing in to tell me?"

"I…guess so."

He watched her, the relaxation ebbing from his stance. "You weren't by any chance coming here to tell me you were quitting? Again?"

Her heart thudded heavily. Joe's stare seemed to swamp her so she couldn't focus on anything except the probing look in his eyes.

"Why are you always so quick to believe the worst of me?"

"Is that what you think I'm doing right now?"

"Well, aren't you?" She lifted her chin, defiant. In her experience, attack was always the best form of defense.

Joe hauled in a deep breath, his undershirt stretching taut across his impressive pectorals. "I'm not wedded to my opinions. I'm prepared to change my mind about you—if you're willing and able to persuade me."

The challenge in his eyes struck sparks in her. The old, familiar recklessness stampeded to the fore, but this time she was rushing in with her eyes wide-open. She knew staying here was a mistake. She knew she should turn around and get out of here. And she knew she was staying because of Joe, because of how he made her feel, all breathless and wired and thrumming and alive—and that was her biggest mistake of all.

But she ignored all the flashing warnings, stared into Joe's wickedly tempting eyes, and said, "Joe, I'm sure if I put my mind to it, I can persuade you into anything."

He sucked in a breath. "Anything in particular?"

The heat in his eyes hit her, made her wonder if she'd gone too far. "What I meant was, changing your opinion of me. I'm not quitting. I'm staying right here."

He rested his forearm against the door frame, leaning into her until his in-your-face masculinity enveloped her. "Are you always such a tease with men? Or is it just me?"

"I don't know what you mean."

"Well, know this. I have my limits. Dangle some bait in front of me long enough and I'll bite."

He leaned in even closer until she thought for sure he was going to kiss her. And she didn't move. Didn't want to move, because all she could think about was his mouth pressing down on hers, scorching and sensuous and thrilling. His shadow fell over her as he closed in, and her heartbeat fluttered in her throat, wild with anticipation…

But then he pulled back, a gleam in his eyes. "Let me know if you have any more trouble with that shower." He walked away, whistling casually.

Dizzy, she stared after his retreating denim-clad ass. Damn him, who was teasing now? And she'd played right into his hands. Why hadn't he kissed her? Why had he pulled back at the last moment? Was it because… Lifting an arm, she gave herself an experimental sniff. Thank God he'd fixed the shower, because she was in desperate need of one.

Chapter Four

Nina stepped out of the shower and wrapped the towel around her body, securing it under her arms. The water had been blissfully hot, and she felt clean and relaxed.

As she padded down the hallway, her footsteps echoed in the hush. The Sunday night crowd at the restaurant and bar had dispersed a while ago. Upstairs, only a handful of guests were staying the night, and they seemed like a quiet bunch.

As she entered her room, a cool breeze struck her damp skin. Earlier in the day, she'd opened the window to air out her room and had forgotten to close it. Now, brisk night air streamed in, raising goose bumps on her arms. She hurried to the sash window and grabbed the brass handles of the raised pane. It wouldn't move. She tugged and wrestled, but the window only screeched down a few inches before jamming again.

"Come on, you stupid thing," she muttered as she tried

to wrench the window down.

The air around her swirled as a warm presence materialized behind her. "Here, let me get that for you." Joe's breath stirred the hairs on her nape.

She spun around. "Jesus, you scared me."

"Sorry. Didn't mean to."

He was mere inches away from her. Too close for comfort, and once again he'd caught her with nothing but a towel on. She edged sideways, keeping her distance from him. "I didn't realize you were still here."

Joe gripped the stuck windowpane and wiggled it from side to side. "I had some paperwork to finish up."

"You seem to spend your whole life here at the inn. Don't you ever have some time off?"

He nudged the pane one more time and drew it closed. "I have time off," he said. "I visit my nonna, sometimes my aunt and uncle, play soccer."

"But you're also here every day."

He secured the window latch and turned back to her. "I built this business up from nothing. I've poured all my time, money, and effort into this place. Of course I'm here every day. I can't afford not to be."

Nina nodded. "I've only been here a few days, but I see how hard you work and how much you've accomplished. I've heard it from your staff, too, and people in town, and, well…I admire what you've achieved and how you've done it."

He blinked, surprise showing in his expression. "Thanks. Didn't think I'd hear you say something like that"—his gaze drifted over her—"let alone do it with nothing but a towel on."

A lick of fire curled in her stomach, sending heat through her veins. "Don't worry," she said. "I'm not trying to seduce you or anything."

His eyes widened, and the corner of his lips twitched. "I'm not against a woman seducing me per se, but in your case I *would* be worried."

"Why?"

Joe shook his head. "You know why." There was an edge to his voice, a warning in his eyes. Was this the same reason he hadn't kissed her yesterday?

"No, I don't." She pinned him with a hard stare. "Come on. You can be honest with me. Am I not attractive enough for you? Is that it?"

He made a kind of choking noise, his eyes flaring. "I wish I could say that, but no. That's not it."

Exhilaration mixed with indignation coursed through her veins. "You sure know how to make a compliment sound like an insult." Her mouth was running away from her again, and she couldn't seem to stop it. Joe was being too provocative to ignore. "Well then? What's your reason?"

"You can't guess?" He paused a moment. "Getting personally involved with you would be…unwise."

His studied deliberation made her feel immature, and she'd had enough of that from her father. She scowled at him. "I see. I'm not *mature* enough for you."

"I didn't say that—"

"Well, you implied it."

He stared back at her for a few moments, his eyes black and inscrutable, before he riffled his fingers through his hair. He groaned. "Why the hell are we even discussing this? No one is going to seduce anyone. Got that?"

"What about yesterday? You almost kissed me—and don't even try to deny it."

"In case you didn't notice, I stopped myself. I have self-control."

His high-handed attitude only made her more reckless. "I see. So the *mature* and *self-controlled* Joe Farina has spoken, and that's it. End of discussion, huh?"

His mouth flattened into a tight line. "Pretty much."

Wildness ran through her, a fierce longing to shake him up and jolt him from his moorings.

"So, I guess if I do *this*—" She ripped off her towel and flung it aside to stand naked in front of Joe. "It won't affect you, then?"

Joe swallowed, his entire body rigid, his dark, fiery gaze eating up every inch of her naked body.

Oh, God, what had she done? This was total madness. What if he reached for her, called her dare? She froze, caught between her impetuosity and Joe's searing examination.

Joe didn't say a word. He just hauled in a harsh breath, eyes black as coal, before he wheeled around and stalked out of her room.

Alone and naked, she felt her insides shrivel to ashes. She'd exposed herself, and Joe had reacted like she was a tantrum-throwing toddler.

Yet Joe was right. She *was* immature for mistaking the strength of his interest in her and thinking he might be overwhelmed with lust for her. She'd been too cocky and full of herself—more faults he'd add to her already lengthy list. Besides, she could hardly call herself an irresistible bombshell. She liked her body, but she wasn't centerfold material, and Joe hadn't had any trouble resisting her.

Her skin felt clammy, and a sharp ache tugged at her belly. Sick at heart, she pulled on clean sweatpants and a baggy sweater, then rumpled the towel over her damp hair while restlessly pacing the room. She'd never be able to fall asleep now. And when she came face-to-face with Joe tomorrow morning, she would die of shame for sure.

She couldn't stand the idea of being tortured all night long. Before she could think twice, she hurried out of her bedroom and down the hall to Joe's office. The door was ajar. Joe stood at the window of his office, looking out with hands on hips, his shoulders broad and stiff. The tension radiating off him was so intimidating Nina was tempted to turn and run before he noticed her. But one thing she'd never lacked was nerve. Better to face him now and get the worst of this messy embarrassment over with. It would still be awkward as hell working with Joe, but at least the initial mortification would be past.

She pushed through the door and walked up to him, her bare feet muffled by the carpet. She was only two feet away when he spun around, his expression freezing as he caught sight of her.

Whatever she was going to say expired in her brain. She spread her arms in a supplicating gesture. "Joe…I, um, wanted to apologize—"

Her words were cut off as he closed the gap between them in one stride and yanked her into his arms. As she landed against his chest, she gasped, all the air knocked out of her by his unexpected move.

"J-Joe?"

Nina barely got the syllable out before his head lowered and his mouth covered hers in a hard, bruising kiss that rocked her foundations. Disbelief stunned her, quickly followed by eager pleasure. His mouth demanded everything from her, and she found herself willingly submitting. The sensation of his hungry lips and his rasping stubble against her skin triggered an instant response. She moved her lips against his, parting them, encouraging him to deepen the kiss, and when his tongue curled into her mouth, she welcomed its possessive heat.

Joe loosened his grip slightly to rove his hands over the back of her sweater before moving down to the hem and slipping under. His wide, callused palms explored the contours of her waist and rib cage, sparking wave upon wave of pleasure across her skin, each one higher, until his hands closed over her bare breasts, and the wave became a tsunami. As he massaged her breasts, slowly and surely, she moaned her gratification against his mouth and arched her back, desire spiraling out of control, panting for more, encouraging him to do whatever he wanted with her.

Joe didn't need a second invitation. He lifted the sweater and pulled it off her. Black eyes glittered in his flushed face as he paused to drink in the sight of her body.

"I can't fight this," he murmured, seemingly to himself, before he lifted her onto his desk, shoving a stack of files to one side.

He pushed her legs apart to fit his body against hers and leaned in to claim her mouth again. His kisses were less frenzied but more demanding, more commanding, and she gave herself up, circling her arms around his neck to pull him closer. While he feasted on her mouth and neck, he cupped her breasts and teased her nipples with his dexterous fingers, making her shudder with excitement and lust.

Heat surged through her. Nothing in the world mattered except this. Joe and his rough kisses and gentle hands. Joe devouring her mouth and teasing her breasts. He transferred his lips from her mouth to her breast, and when he sucked hard she couldn't breathe for the exquisite pleasure he gave her. How could he know so perfectly how to turn her on? He grazed the edge of his teeth against her nipple, and a line of fire streaked from her breast straight to the throbbing ache between her thighs. She was already wet for him. If he kept on sucking her breasts she would orgasm right there and then.

But, as if he knew and wanted to torment her, he released her nipple and began to lick the valley between her breasts. The sensation was novel to her, and she clutched his shoulders for support. Joe's thick black hair tickled her breasts as he slowly inched his way down toward her belly button.

Instinctively she wrapped her legs around his hips and pulled him into her. As his groin made contact with her, the unmistakable bulge in his pants pressed up between her thighs, perfectly poised at her entrance. *Holy mother…* Her brain almost fried as she registered his size and hardness and position. Just two layers of fabric lay between them.

The image of Joe's erection triggered the first stirrings of panic. Any moment now Joe would slide his hand inside her pants, and once he touched her down there she'd be lost. She'd agree to everything and anything he wanted. *Anything.* There wasn't anything she couldn't imagine doing with Joe, and that was pretty damn exciting—but at the same time it was out-of-this-world scary.

Alarmed, she pushed an arm out and knocked over a

mug filled with pens. It thudded to the ground, the noise breaking the spell. Joe's head lifted from her stomach. His hazy eyes fixed on her, and she could almost see his rationality returning. Blinking, he slowly straightened, his hands falling away from her, and chilly air cooled the fire that burned in her. She pushed herself off the desk and, with a belated rush of modesty, crossed her arms over her breasts. Talk about shutting the stable door after the horse had bolted.

Without a word, Joe retrieved her sweater from the floor and carefully pulled it over her head, helping her arms into the sleeves like she was a three-year-old.

"I'm sorry," he said, his voice wooden. "I shouldn't have done that."

He was still treating her as if she were an immature child and he the responsible adult. That wasn't fair. She grimaced at him. "Why not? I enjoyed it."

His hands curled into fists. "As usual, you're not considering the big picture. You're my employee. I *never, ever* cross the line with my employees. It's unprofessional and unethical, and it can lead to messy, expensive sexual harassment claims, which I really don't need."

"I don't see the problem." She'd been alarmed at how quickly things had heated up between them, but now that he'd drawn back, perversely she wished he hadn't. "It's not like I'm going to sue you."

"How do I know that for sure?"

"Because…" She didn't need the money or the bad publicity, but Joe didn't know that. "Because I wouldn't."

"That's so reassuring," he snapped sarcastically. "But besides that, it's also bad for my other employees if they see me fooling around with you."

"No one saw us."

Joe's face darkened. "And you're forgetting the biggest reason of all—you're bad for my concentration, and I *never, ever* repeat the same mistake."

She scowled back at him. "I'm getting sick of your *never, ever* rules. Why can't we have some fun? We're not hurting anyone."

"And that's all this is? Some harmless fun?"

"Sure." She widened her eyes at him. He wasn't the only one who could be sarcastic. "I'm not expecting you to fall in l-love with me."

Shoot, why had she stammered on the word "love," as if it meant something to her?

A wary look shadowed Joe's face. "You can't say it, can you?"

"Can *you*?" Instantly she was back on the offense.

"I have no intentions of saying that word." He backed away as if she were a live grenade. "Christ, how did this conversation end up here?"

"You kissed me, and we both liked it, but you don't want to take it any further."

"God, Nina. You're such a…a minx, it's too hard to think straight around you, but you need to know I mean what I say."

Joe pushed his fingers through his hair, making it even more tousled and sexy. Nina's heart contracted in an odd spasm. Why did every little thing about Joe affect her so much?

She gave herself a shake and straightened her sweater. "Fine, if you say so. I'm not that hot at seduction anyway."

He blinked, as if he hadn't expected her cooperation,

and gave her a lopsided, sexy smile. "I wouldn't say that, but I'm glad we agree on something."

She ignored the melting sensation his smile invoked. "We won't do it again. This was a one-time incident that won't be repeated."

"Remember that the next time you feel like dropping your towel and parading naked in front of me." He paused, a smile tugging at the corners of his mouth. "There's only so much temptation a man can take, you know."

"Well, I only did that because you were being so annoying."

He raised his eyebrows. "Is that how you normally deal with annoying men?"

"You're a special case."

"I'm glad I'm special."

Her stomach tingled again. Uh-oh. The buzz Joe was giving her was bad news. Just moments ago they'd agreed not to act on the attraction between them, but then immediately she couldn't help flirting with him. And he was flirting with her, too, no mistaking that.

"I'm going to bed," she said, backing away from him.

Joe nodded. "Good night, then. You should have an easier day tomorrow. Mondays the restaurant and bar are closed, and we don't have any guests booked for the night. After you've cleaned the rooms, you can take the rest of the day off and relax."

I definitely need a break, Nina thought as she made her way back to her bedroom. But if Joe was going to be around, she doubted she'd be able to relax.

. . .

Heat flushed through Joe, raising a light sweat on the back of his neck. His heart rate quickened as if he were jogging, but all he'd done was catch sight of Nina sunbathing in the courtyard next to the bar. The weather was unexpectedly warm, and she wore a loose orange T-shirt and tight black leggings. Stretched out on a wooden bench, she exuded a feline grace that had Joe's attention shackled.

Earlier, he'd tried to do some paperwork in his office, but his concentration had evaporated as soon as he'd sat at his desk and been reminded in vivid detail what he and Nina had done on that slab of wood. His memories had refused to subside, along with the bulge in his groin that throbbed insistently as he remembered the hot, silky feel of Nina's body writhing beneath him. Distracted and frustrated, he'd gone to the bar to get himself a can of Coke, but only succeeded in fanning the fire when he spotted Nina outside.

As he watched, Nina arched her toes. The curve of her bare feet transfixed him; he wanted to run his fingers over her delicate ankles, then wrap her legs around his hips before burying... His palm burned against the cool Coke can. Before he could reconsider, he grabbed a second soda can from behind the bar and walked out into the courtyard.

Nina sat up, her expression edgy as he approached.

"Want a soda?" He offered one of the cans to her.

"Uh, sure." She took it gingerly, as if afraid to make physical contact with him.

The kinetic buzz between them clearly wasn't one-sided. Maybe she also couldn't stop thinking about last night. Drawing her knees up, she motioned to him to sit beside her. He perched on the edge of the bench and popped the tab of his drink, not able to relax with her slender, Lycra-clad legs so close to him.

Tension hummed from Nina as she circled the top of her soda can with her fingertip. She darted a glance at him, opened her mouth as if about to say something, then closed it.

The inn was deserted, and a vine-covered trellis screened the courtyard from the street. A gentle breeze rustled the leaves.

Joe cleared his throat. "Nice weather we're having."

She nodded. "Yeah, it's beautiful today."

Christ. They'd been reduced to discussing the weather, and all because of what had happened. He turned to face her.

"Look, about last night. We have to put it behind us. We both did some stupid things—you dropping your towel, and me reacting like a..." He groped for the right description of the tremendous force that had gripped him last night, which was still heaving just beneath the surface. "A caveman."

Yeah, as soon as he'd clapped eyes on Nina's naked body, a primitive urge to ravish her had all but overpowered him. Only by stomping out of the room had he managed to control himself, but when she'd followed him to his office, he hadn't been able to help himself kissing her, caressing her, and only a minor miracle had stopped him from taking her right there on his office desk.

"A caveman." Nina's lips curved into a small, delicious smile.

His groin stirred. He shook his head. "You're doing it again."

"Doing what?"

"You've got to stop this"—he flicked a finger between

them—"this flirting."

"I'm not flirting with you." Indignation flared in her vivid blue eyes.

"You just gave me a coy smile and said 'caveman' in a breathy voice. That's flirting."

She swung her legs to the ground and sat up, her spine ramrod straight. "Sounds like wishful thinking on your part. I know when I'm flirting with a guy, and I damn well was not flirting with you. If I smiled at all when I said 'caveman,' it's only because I was thinking what a good caveman you'd make, what with all that lovely, thick hair of yours and your broad shoulders and your big, muscly arms…" Her voice trailed off. She sucked in her lower lip, looking guilty. "Okay, I admit that last part was a bit flirty."

Joe let out a groan. "For Christ's sakes, woman. Can you please stop? I'm not made of stone, you know."

Chuckling, she lined her legs together. "I promise to behave. As long as you do." She took a sip of Coke.

He stared at her moistened lips, and the ache to suck the soda off her mouth corkscrewed his insides. "You're bad for me, Nina. You make me want to do stupid things."

"And you always do the smart thing?"

"I thought I did." Dating Deanne had seemed like the smart thing to do at the time. He'd known her since high school, and she knew his family, his responsibilities. He'd assumed they were well matched, but look how wrong he'd been there.

Nina shifted on the bench. "For the record, I wanted to kiss you the moment I laid eyes on you." Color glowed in her cheeks as she peeped at him through her eyelashes.

"Yeah?" He was ashamed at how much her confession

gratified him.

"Uh-huh." She smiled again. "There's something about you that's so dark and irresistible. Plus, you do have a gorgeous body, what I've seen of it, and those lips of yours, oh, mama!"

Heaven help him, but there was only so much a man could withstand.

I'm going to regret this, but what the hell…

Leaning forward, he captured her hand and pressed his mouth into her palm, keeping his gaze on hers. She gasped, the blue in her eyes deepening, challenging him. When he flicked the tip of his tongue against her hand, her entire body shivered. Coke cans clattered to the ground as he pulled her closer, his animal hunger breaking free. He laid a trail of quick kisses across her palm before transferring his attention to her neck. Nina arched her back to accommodate him, her little moans guiding him to all her delightful, sensitive spots.

Her mouth lured him, but he held himself back, wanting to spin out the anticipation, to tease them both a little, knowing that when he finally kissed her lips, fireworks would explode.

But just as he couldn't hold out any longer, a beeping cell phone interrupted them. He hesitated, cursing the interruption and wanting to ignore it. But Nina was already stretching away from him as she picked up her phone from the bench.

Her expression was half dazed, but when she answered the call, she instantly snapped to attention, the bliss wiped off her face.

"Dad? Oh my God, is it really you?" She scrambled

away from Joe, tugging at the hem of her T-shirt. "I, um, I wasn't expecting to hear from you."

Goddammit. Why hadn't he kissed her while he had the chance? Seconds ago Nina's body had been soft and supple, but now she was stiff, her rising tension palpable. She took a few steps away from the bench as the conversation continued. Joe's body cooled fast. Nothing like an unexpected call from her father to ruin the fun.

Nina sounded agitated on the phone. She paused a long while, listening intently. After a few minutes she muttered good-bye and slipped the phone into the pocket of her T-shirt.

"That was my dad," she said unnecessarily, dragging her fingers through her mussed-up hair. She seemed at a loss for words, and Joe recalled something she'd mentioned a couple of days ago.

"Is he the family problem you touched on earlier?"

Nina chewed on her lower lip, clearly debating whether to confide in him, and he found himself hoping she would.

"Um, yes." She hesitated again. "Can I tell you something?"

Joe nodded. "Of course."

"I came to Hartley to get away from my father."

"Why?" His fists clenched as he jerked upright. "Is he abusing you or something?"

"No, nothing like that." She shook her head quickly. "We just don't see eye to eye. He's controlling, and I… Well, I don't take kindly to his interference." She paused to swallow, and he could have sworn he caught a glimpse of tears in her eyes before she looked away. "Something happened the other day, and it was the last straw. I couldn't take it anymore. So I left."

Joe frowned as he digested Nina's confession. "You left? Caught the first bus out of San Francisco?"

She pursed her lips and nodded.

Suspicion rose as the truth dawned on him. "Hang on. You weren't the person I was waiting for that day you arrived, were you?"

Nina lifted her shoulders in admission. "No."

He pushed to his feet. "Why didn't you tell me?"

"You didn't give me a chance. You rushed me inside and shoved a mop and bucket at me before I could say anything."

"Don't give me that. You had plenty of time to tell me the truth, but you didn't. You deliberately misled me."

"No, not really. My intention was to find a job here. It just so happened that I walked into one completely by accident, and the person who was meant to show up never arrived. Why are you mad at me? You needed a maid, and I turned up. What's wrong with that? It's a win-win situation."

"It's anything but." He glared at her, not exactly sure why he was so riled. Maybe because he hated being duped. Maybe because within five minutes of meeting Nina, he'd wanted her. Still wanted her, even now. That made him more annoyed. "If you lied to get this job, what else have you lied about? What else should I know about you?"

A beat of silence passed. Something flickered in her eyes. Was it guilt or anxiety?

Then she drew herself upright, hair gleaming in the sunlight. "You know all you have to know. I don't owe you my entire life history."

Hell. One minute she was melting in his arms and the next she was proud and uppity. And goddammit if that didn't make her even hotter. He burned to bend her over his arm and silence that pouty mouth of hers with his. Lust flared in him, and for a moment he teetered on the edge of giving in, before he pulled back.

"Fine," he conceded, muscles tensed against the temptation to grab her. "As long as you don't lie anymore. From now on, you have to be honest with me. Got it?"

. . .

Nina gulped hard. Joe's gaze was so penetrating she had an irrational fear he could see what was milling in her head. Should she tell him who her dad was and what he'd done? But if she did, then that would negate her whole reason for being here. She couldn't tell him she was Carson Beaumont's daughter, that on her recent twenty-fifth birthday she'd come into a trust fund worth millions, and that, despite all her privileges and advantages, she couldn't command the respect of her colleagues. She couldn't tell him. Not until she'd achieved what she'd come here to prove to herself. The minute Joe knew her true identity, this life experiment of hers would bust. She needed to see it through, even if that meant lying about not lying.

"Got it," she said.

They looked at each other, and the heat between them began to build again. Her lips quivered as she relived how close Joe had come to kissing her before her dad's call had interrupted them. God, how she wanted to feel his mouth on hers again. Even when they were arguing, she couldn't stop wanting him. Joe's brand of aggravation was somehow arousing.

His mocha eyes reflected the fire leaping between them,

his lids dropping to half-mast as he focused on her lips. But then he seemed to come to his senses and took a step back, his stance relaxing.

He angled his head in the direction of the street. "Want to go for a drive?"

She started at his non sequitur. "Excuse me?"

"There're some beautiful spots around these parts, and you haven't seen much since you arrived."

"You honestly want to take me sightseeing?"

He let out a small sigh, his lips quirking at the corners. "Don't overthink it, Nina."

What was there to think about? He wasn't pushing her away. He still wanted to be with her. "I'd love to." She smiled back at him.

A short while later, she was sitting in Joe's blue pickup truck while he drove them along a narrow road that hugged the coastline. Sunshine glinted on the nearby ocean and lifted Nina's spirits. It was a beautiful day, and she was spending it with a gorgeous man. What could be better?

Joe eased back in his seat, hands relaxed on the steering wheel, and glanced at her. "So. Care to tell me about that phone call from your father?"

Tension flowed back, but she did owe Joe some sort of explanation. Preferably one as close to the truth as possible. "He was checking up on me, as usual."

Her father had wanted to talk about her promotion, but she'd stalled him. He and that promotion weren't subjects dear to her heart. "He's probably just being protective," Joe said.

"There's more. He reminded me that my stepsister's wedding is coming up in three weeks."

"I see. And you're going to be a bridesmaid?"

Nina choked. "Hell, no. I look awful in frilly dresses, and Brooke wouldn't want me in her bridal party."

"So…no love lost between you two, huh?"

"Nope. Brooke and I are complete opposites."

Meaning Brooke was the spotless, perfect daughter her dad had always wanted. Nina was fifteen when her dad had married Ellen, a well-connected socialite who never had a hair out of place, and brought her and her daughter, Brooke, to live with him and Nina. Ellen had lost no time waving her decorating wand over the entire house, eradicating every sign of Nina's late mother. Nina was quite happy to hate her new stepmother.

And then there was Brooke, one year her senior and superior to her in every way that mattered to her dad. Brooke was a straight-A student, class president, captain of the debating team, and she never cursed, drank, smoked, or cut class. Or, if she did, she was way better at hiding it than Nina. Her father doted on Brooke, and when he adopted her and gave her the Beaumont surname, to Nina it felt as if he'd finally gotten the daughter he'd always wanted.

With Brooke set to marry the son of a senator, Nina was more than happy to fade into the background, hoping even to skip the event, which had been billed the party of the decade. Lavish society weddings were so not her, especially with the memory of her two-faced ex-boyfriend still fresh in her mind.

"I really don't want to go," she said to Joe.

"But they're your family. You have to."

"Humph. You don't know *my* family."

"What's so special about your family?"

Trepidation danced down her spine. She wasn't ready to confess to Joe she was a Beaumont. She felt bad lying to him, but she'd feel even worse if she told him the truth and saw his attitude toward her alter. People always treated her differently, once they knew who she was and how much money she had.

"They're difficult," she said. "And not just my dad, but also my stepmom and my stepsister."

"You mentioned earlier your mom passed away." He offered a sympathetic look. "How long ago was that again?"

"She died when I was thirteen. Dad remarried two years later."

"Can't have been easy for you. But you're no cakewalk either." His voice held a teasing smile. "I'd say you gave as much as you got."

"Or more," Nina admitted.

"Families aren't always easy, are they?"

Minutes later, Joe pulled off the road and parked the truck in a small clearing. She followed him through the scrub until they came to a rocky cove, where glistening dark rocks tumbled down to a deep cerulean ocean.

"Oh, it's beautiful!" she exclaimed, gazing down at the seawater that swirled and crashed against the boulders.

"I used to come here all the time when I was a teenager. When the winter storms hit it's amazing to see the waves crashing against the cliffs."

"Look over there." Nina pointed farther below at a ledge of rock jutting out high over the water. Three teenage boys stood on the platform, and as she watched, one of them leaped off the edge, whooping as he disappeared. "Are they insane?"

"I've done that plenty of times," Joe assured her. "It's safe as long as the sea's not too rough. Come on, let's take a closer look."

As he led her down to the ledge, the two other boys jumped off, too, hollering and cackling. When they reached the rock platform, Nina peeped over the edge. Wow, the ocean was a long way down, at least thirty feet or more. Below, the three teenagers swam for the water's edge, whooping and high-fiving.

Nina turned back to Joe. "Well? Are you game?"

"What?" he said before comprehension dawned on his face. "Oh… No, I don't think so."

"Why not?"

"I only brought you here for the view. I haven't jumped off that cliff in ages."

"Okay, old man. I'll go on my own." She started kicking off her Crocs.

Joe stared at her. "You're serious?"

"If those boys can do it, so can I." She rolled off her black leggings, pausing when she caught Joe's eye. "What? I'm not taking everything off, and besides, it's not as if you haven't seen the full buffet already."

He muttered something under his breath. It might have been a curse word. She turned away from him and edged toward the precipice. Her heart revved in her chest. She was nervous about the jump, but she wanted to have some fun. *Needed* some pure, mindless joy in her life. If Joe didn't want to make out with her, then jumping off a cliff was the next best thing. She shuffled forward, filling her lungs with the fresh, briny air as her body tingled with excitement.

"Wait," Joe ordered. There was a faint clink of a belt

being unbuckled, and when she turned she almost swooned at the sight of Joe standing in just his black boxer briefs, his jeans, T-shirt, and shoes discarded.

Oh, oh, *oh*. She couldn't focus on anything except his abs, his arms, his waist. That package snugly encased in tight black cotton. Good God, she needed oxygen.

He plucked at her T-shirt. "Take that off, too. You'll need something dry to wear afterward."

She nodded, wordless, and obeyed. When she was stripped down to bra and panties, Joe appeared to have a hard time looking elsewhere, too.

He swallowed hard, and then he took her hand and nodded down at the ocean below. "We'll jump on three. Ready?"

She nodded again. The feel of his fingers wrapped around hers and the tickle of his arm against hers sent the adrenaline soaring. Holding hands with Joe felt even more exciting than jumping off this cliff.

"One, two, three!"

She didn't stop shrieking as they plummeted down. Her senses were assaulted by the rushing wind, the feel of Joe's body falling with her, and her own weightlessness. They plunged into the ocean, and cold water seized her. Bubbles filled her vision before she kicked her way to the surface, popping up at the same time as Joe.

She let out a few whoops of exhilaration. "That was awesome!"

Joe wore a big grin on his face. "Yeah. I'm surprised I can still hear."

She splashed some water at him and laughed. "Admit it. You enjoyed it, too."

"I did." Moving closer, he wrapped his arms around her. "You're a very bad influence on me."

His chest pressed up against her breasts, and suddenly there was a lot more to get excited about. But just then a wave slapped into them, dragging them under for a few seconds.

"Let's get out before we freeze to death," Joe said when they reemerged.

He kept beside her as they swam toward the rocks and scrambled out of the water.

Nina stood shivering on the damp rocks, not regretting one moment of the experience.

"Those teenagers aren't far away," Joe said. "They're not going to move while you're showing all that." With a lazy smile he dropped his gaze to her chest, and she saw that her white bra was now practically transparent and her nipples had pebbled from the cold.

She swallowed. The heat in Joe's look made her nipples even harder and achy for his touch.

She drew in a breath and waved at the teenagers. "Hiya, boys!" They gawped and waved timidly back, looking skinny and raw compared to the alpha male next to her. But when she turned back to Joe, he was already heading up to the rock platform, so she fell in behind him.

Watching Joe's ass clad in wet boxer briefs was no hardship at all. All too soon, they arrived back at their clothes, where Joe dressed with brisk efficiency. She would have liked to linger for a while, maybe watch the sun set, but it was obvious Joe was eager to get back to the inn. He'd already spent more time than he'd bargained taking her out for a drive, so she couldn't complain.

They drove back to town in companionable silence.

"Thanks for taking me there," she said when they entered the Comet Inn. "I really enjoyed myself."

"I'm glad. Hartley's full of hidden gems like that. You just have to know where they are."

"Maybe you could show me another one next Monday."

Joe paused and gave her a sharp, assessing look. She didn't care for that look—it always seemed to conclude in some deficiency on her part.

"Or any other Monday would do, too," she added, trying to force a response from him.

"You're planning on sticking around, then?"

Oh, yes, she'd been right about that look of his. She propped one hand on her hip as she faced him fully. "Why wouldn't I?"

"You have a wedding in San Francisco in three weeks."

"What are you implying?"

Joe pushed his fingers through his salt-stiffened hair. "I'm not implying anything, but look at it from my point of view. You might be pissed off with your dad, but he wants you at your sister's wedding. Add to that the fact you're not used to small-town living and you're not exactly thrilled with your job here, and, well...I'd be a fool to assume you'd stick out your probation period."

His cool, dispassionate reasoning made her clench her fists. "I'm not a quitter. I might have to go to my *step*sister's wedding, but it's just one weekend. It's not going to change my plan. I'll be back."

But that was impossible, she realized with a pang. She had to be in San Francisco before Brooke's wedding. With her vacation time used up, she'd have to return to her job at

Beaumont, Inc. She *was* returning, wasn't she? This whole working-as-a-maid thing was strictly temporary. But if she told Joe that, why would he keep her on?

"You're sure?" he said. "One weekend in the big city might remind you of everything you've been missing."

"I said I'll be back," she reiterated through gritted teeth.

"Why? Because of…this?" He waggled his finger. "This *thing* between us?"

She drew herself up. "It's not just the URST. I have things to prove to myself, too."

"The URST?"

"Unresolved sexual tension. What you call 'this thing.'"

He blinked, and then a rueful smile spread across his face. "It's true I've been URSTing after you something bad."

"Well? What are you going to do about it?"

Silence hung over the deserted lobby. He cupped her cheek in one hand, concentrating on her mouth for so long she felt breathless. "There are so many things I want to do…"

He brushed his thumb across her lower lip, and she was held captive like a bee in nectar. "You like to keep a girl in suspense, don't you?" Her words came out unsteady, needy.

"No. You're a special case, Nina. I've never met anyone like you."

Her heart flipped a somersault, painfully, and suddenly all her sass dried up, and she could only stare mutely at him, waiting for him to make the next move, to kiss her. Because surely he wanted to kiss her? Surely he wanted to finish what he'd started before that ill-timed call from her dad?

But instead of kissing her, he lowered his hand from her, and she was left wondering, aching.

"I have to get back to my bookkeeping," he said.

"What?"

"I still have a lot of receipts to get through."

Bookkeeping? Receipts? He'd rather do bookkeeping and receipts than kiss her?

"Oh…" What little confidence she had left whooshed out of her like a leaking balloon.

"We'll talk later."

What did that mean? Was "talk" code for "make out"? She wished she knew; she wished she had the guts to ask him.

"O-okay."

She pressed her lips together as she watched Joe cross the lobby and head back to his office. If she were Nina Summers without a dime to her name, she would've run after him, crash-tackled him to the floor, if necessary. But underneath it all she was still Annette Beaumont, and there seemed to be no getting away from that.

Chapter Five

The wicker chair on the balcony looked so inviting. And Nina's muscles were crying for a break after her lengthy stint of cleaning made even harder by the fitful sleep she'd endured last night, tortured by dreams of Joe naked except for those black boxer briefs.

Nina pressed a hand into the aching small of her back and uttered a groan. *Just five minutes*, she told herself as she eased down on the cushions of the wicker chair. Mmm, it was so comfy here with the gentle midmorning sun bathing her and a view of Hartley and the ocean spread out in front of her. Just five minutes rest and she'd feel like new again. Her limbs relaxed, and her eyelids drooped…

Someone tapped her on the shoulder, and she jackknifed up, surprised and disoriented.

"What's going on?"

She squinted up to see Joe towering over her, looking displeased. Her heart dropped as she scrambled to her feet.

"Um, I was just, uh, taking care of a few cobwebs." She grabbed the broom that had fallen to the floor.

"Oh, yeah? Looked more like taking a few z's."

A guilty blush heated her cheeks. Shoot, just yesterday she'd insisted she was staying put, and now he'd caught her napping on the job.

"I-I'm sorry." She edged back from him and leaned against the balcony railing. "It won't happen again. It's just that I didn't get much sleep last night."

"Still worrying about your dad?"

The unexpected concern in his voice made her pause. "Not really. I mean, we have issues, but it's nothing new."

"So if it's not that, then what's been keeping you up at night?"

Memories of yesterday danced through her mind—Joe's suntanned body brushing against hers on that stone ledge, the thrill of jumping with him, his fingers interlaced with hers. And earlier, that kiss that had almost happened, that she still wanted so badly. *That* was what had kept her up last night.

"You," she blurted. "I can't stop thinking about you."

Oh my God, what is wrong with my mouth? It seemed it had a will of its own.

Joe's eyes widened. "Me?"

"You and the URST. It's driving me crazy." Huh. Yes, she had officially lost control of her mouth.

"Ah, the URST. Yeah, there's a lot of that going around at the moment."

She could have sworn there was a glint in his eyes. Her pulse was racing, her fingers twitching. Nervous, she licked her lips, and Joe seemed to be riveted by her action. She stepped closer to him, and there was no mistaking the increase in his breathing rate.

"You too?" she asked, emboldened by his reaction to her.

She was close enough to feel his body heat and inhale his clean, masculine scent. Even in the pitch dark she'd be able to pick him out. She closed her eyes, imagining herself blindfolded in a bedroom with Joe, and the potency of her fantasy made her sway.

"Nina." Joe's gruff voice made her open her eyes. The pent-up hunger in his expression made her lungs constrict. A look like that could melt a girl's panties off.

"Yeah?"

She swayed closer, the need to touch him overwhelming. She rested a hand against his chest and it was like touching a live generator. He pressed his palm over hers, his grip hard and urgent. Sunshine glinted off his dark, wavy hair, picked out the faint lines at the corners of his fierce eyes. Her heart leaped in her throat. *My God, he's so gorgeous…*

"Yoo-hoo!" A voice from below trilled, bursting the bubble that had enclosed them. "Good morning, Joe. Good morning, Nina. Isn't it a lovely day?"

Mrs. Stewart. Standing on the sidewalk and gazing up at them. And calling out for everyone in the street to know that Joe and Nina were together.

Joe pulled away from Nina as he returned Mrs. Stewart's greeting. Nina wasn't capable of speech, so she waved instead. Mrs. Stewart nodded and smiled before trotting on down the street.

"We need to talk." His clipped tone felt like a jab to the stomach.

. . .

Joe shut the balcony doors firmly behind Nina, cursing his weakness. Christ, what had Mrs. Stewart seen from the street below? Had she noticed the dangerous hunger in him as he held Nina's hand and imagined all the ways he wanted to rip her clothes off?

He should've been mad at her for sleeping on the job, but all he'd wanted to do was to kiss those soft strawberry lips. And that was another reason why he had to resist temptation—it wasn't professional or fair to his other employees if he gave her preferential treatment just because he was desperate to sleep with her. He had to be firm before she made him look like a complete sap. And that might have happened already since Mrs. Stewart had caught them holding hands, him probably looking moonstruck and idiotic. She was a sweet lady but the biggest gossip in town, and God knew whom she'd already told.

Nina was studying him with a slightly apprehensive expression. He was uneasy, too. Nina was about as predictable as a tornado.

"I've been thinking. About us." The words jerked out of him.

"Okay…" she said, caution clouding the fire in her eyes.

"We shouldn't fool around or flirt with each other anymore. We should go back to being just friends." Clearly there was no way they'd ever go back to being boss and employee, if they ever had been in the first place.

She stared at him, clearly perplexed. "I have to point out that we aren't actually friends."

"I took you for a drive yesterday. I jumped into the sea with you." And he'd never felt more alive and carefree as when they'd hurtled through the air, hand in hand, Nina's shrieks of joy echoing his exhilaration. "Doesn't that count?"

"Maybe…" She tilted her head. "And when you say friends, you don't mean friends with benefits?"

"No," he retorted. "I mean platonic friends." But there'd been nothing platonic in his reaction to seeing her step out of the sea with her semitransparent bra clinging to her breasts, her perky nipples provocatively outlined. If it hadn't been for those gawking teenage boys, he wasn't sure he could have resisted temptation. No, they definitely weren't platonic friends yet, but he could work at it.

"Why?" Nina asked.

"Why?" He widened his eyes at her. "Because it's better this way. All this flirting going on between us can't stay secret forever. I don't want it upsetting the rest of the staff and, to be frank, it's messing with my concentration, too. I've got a lot to deal with at the moment—the inn, my new business, my grandmother, the Food and Wine Festival."

Plus, he didn't have time to find a replacement for Nina. Yesterday he'd contacted the employment agency and discovered the person they were supposed to have sent him had changed her mind at the last minute, but the agency hadn't bothered to notify him, which meant he wasn't using that agency again.

"Right." Nina pressed her hands to her hips and glowered at him. "So I'm just an inconvenient little itch that's screwing up your wonderful, busy world."

Little itch? That was hardly the right description for the raging lust she induced in him, but that wasn't the point.

"There's your dad, too."

Her brows drew together. "My dad? What's he got to do with anything?"

"You obviously have problems with him. Your life is complicated enough without adding a secret…" He waved his hand impatiently. "Affair."

"That's bull. You're reaching for excuses."

"I'm sorry. I shouldn't have led you on. But it's better this way."

She glared at him, eyes blazing, and despite the situation, he couldn't help admiring the obstinate line of her jaw and the feisty set of her lips. Even when she was angry with him she was such a turn-on.

"Right," she said. "It's *so* much better now that you've toyed with me and dropped me without any discussion."

"I'm discussing it right now."

"No, you're not. You've already made up your mind, and now you want to deliver the bad news pronto and scuttle off like a cockroach."

Shit, the woman had a tongue like a razor. "If you want to take a shot at me, then go ahead. I'm not scuttling off anywhere."

"How big of you." Nina ran her fingers through her hair, pushing up sheaves of golden strands. "But don't worry. I'm not going to have a huge meltdown just because you're tired of me."

Tired of Nina? Was that even possible?

She tugged at her T-shirt, stretching the material across her bust, and for a moment he was blinded by the memory of her breasts—sweet and delicate, with delicious nipples that responded so well to his licking…

Need roiled in him to grasp her and make a mockery of everything he'd just said. He shut his eyes and growled as he strove for willpower.

"I'll be as nice as pie to everyone." Her glower singed him, taunting him as it fueled his hunger. "Even you." The air between them beat with prickling silence. Then she straightened her shoulders and walked away, leaving him alone, aroused, and uneasy.

• • •

Joe was restless. It was Wednesday night, and the local wine club was having its monthly meeting in the restaurant. Normally Joe enjoyed chatting with the members, but tonight he couldn't settle and instead prowled back and forth between the bar and the restaurant.

If he'd thought reining in his lust for Nina would restore normality to his life, then he was sorely disappointed. Ever since yesterday morning Nina had treated him with a shiny brightness that grated because he knew it was meant to irritate him. When she'd turned that friendliness on others—whether it was the guests, the staff, or anyone else who turned up at the inn—he'd been forced to watch them bask in her warmth. He'd grit his teeth until he had a permanent ache in his jawbone.

Tonight she was busing tables in the restaurant, and because he didn't want her thinking that he was checking up on her, he ducked in and out from the bar next door. As the evening wore on, he walked into the restaurant one more time to see Nina standing by the counter that displayed the club's featured bottles of wine.

"These are some good wines you have here," Joe heard Nina say to the president of the wine club.

The guy went pink with pleasure. "We try to get a good variety."

"That 1997 Barbaresco is very nice." She pointed to one of the bottles.

The president raised his eyebrows. "Yes, isn't it?" He coughed, clearly taken aback. "A wine for special occasions."

Joe was just as surprised as the president. How was a lowly coffee shop waitress familiar with wine that cost more than a hundred and fifty bucks a bottle?

Nina caught Joe's eye and flushed as if she'd been caught. "Oh, er, maybe I was mistaken."

She picked up her tray and rushed off, glasses clinking dangerously. Joe followed her into the wash area of the kitchen.

"So you're a wine aficionado, eh?"

Sarah, who'd been walking past, stopped. "Who's a wine aficionado?"

"Nina." Joe nodded in her direction. "Apparently she likes a drop of 1997 Barbaresco."

"What?" Sarah eyed Nina suspiciously. "How can you afford a wine like that?"

Nina noisily rinsed the glasses. "I never said I'd bought it. I just know how to, you know, sound knowledgeable about it." She waved a hand, scattering water droplets over them. "It's all about the elegant palate and the raspberry notes and the abundant tannin and—"

"Okay, I've heard enough." Sarah walked off.

Joe continued to study Nina. He couldn't figure her out. Had she been flirting with the president of the wine club just to get a rise out of him? Or did she really drink expensive wine?

"When you're done here, there're some tables in the bar that need clearing," he said.

He left and returned to the bar, where he vowed not to let Nina affect him anymore. But that didn't stop his neck muscles from bunching up when she entered the bar and went to clear a table where a group of men was sitting. The men started chatting with her, and she responded, looking so relaxed and friendly that Joe found himself gritting his teeth again. With a final smile, Nina picked up her tray, and as she walked off, all the guys at the table swiveled as one to check out her ass. Joe clenched his fists until they felt like boulders hanging at his sides. How dare those dickwads stare at her like that?

Still simmering dangerously, he marched over to the bar where Nina was sliding her tray across to Vince.

"Having fun?" he bit out.

She spun around at his sharp tone. Vince raised his eyebrows at him, but all Joe's attention was focused on the maddening woman in front of him.

"I am," she smoothly replied.

Nina was in the black denim jeans and lemon sweater he'd seen her in many times before, but despite that and the fact she'd been working several hours, she'd never seemed more luscious and irresistible. Why was it so hard to stick to his guns?

"Things are winding down," he said. "Why don't you quit early?"

She raised her eyebrows. "But my shift doesn't end for another hour."

Another hour of watching her strut around the place giving all the male customers something to pant over? His blood vessels wouldn't survive that. "I'll cover for you. You can have an early night. Don't worry, I'll still pay you for the full shift."

She tapped her fingernails on the bar counter. "I'm not worried."

"No, nothing's worrying you today, apparently."

A muscle twitched in her cheek. "That's right. I'm peachy keen."

"I can see that. So can everyone else. Especially that group of guys you were just batting your eyelashes at."

Blue fire sparked in her eyes as she leaned toward him. "Jealous? Would you prefer I bat my eyelashes at you?"

Her scent filled his nostrils. She smelled of honeysuckle and hand-cut potato wedges and a hint of beer—a knockout combination that made him want to pull her to his chest. The force of his urges made him dizzy. He glanced about, wondering if anyone was witnessing his turmoil, and saw Vince had retreated to the other end of the bar counter, where he busied himself polishing a glass as if his life depended on it.

"Look." Joe jerked his chin. "We've scared Vince away."

"*You've* scared him away. I haven't done anything."

"The hell you haven't. Ever since yesterday you've been flouncing around in front of me, wiggling your ass in my face."

"Wiggling!" Several people looked up. Nina flung down her dishcloth, lowering her voice as she said, "Why would I wiggle and flounce at you? You've made it clear you don't want my ass anywhere near your face."

Blood thudded in his ears. Maybe holding back wasn't

such a good idea after all. For a start, it was bad for his blood pressure. And how could he concentrate on anything if he constantly had to fight his urges? And battle his raging jealousy every time Nina so much as smiled at another guy? If this frustration continued for much longer, he'd explode, and probably at the worst possible time. Better to find a safety valve and release some pressure, right?

He butted in and shoved his elbow on the counter next to her, pressing his forearm against hers. She let out a little gasp as her flesh quivered against his. He was quivering, too, the contact with her skin firing every brain synapse. Her blue eyes, big as saucers, sucked him in.

Yeah, he needed that safety valve real bad right now.

Joe bent his head toward Nina's. "Meet me out back in half an hour," he whispered, "and I'll show you where to put your ass."

A pulse fluttered in her throat as she swallowed. She moistened her lips, her face flushed and fierce. "You'd better show up," she huffed, her voice low and hoarse, "or I'll never speak to you again, Joe Farina."

He gave her a brash grin. "Now that's the kind of win-win proposition I like."

• • •

This could be a disaster in so many ways.

As Nina headed for the door that led to the rear of the inn, she considered running back to her room, but her body had a will of its own, and her feet continued down the hallway.

She was setting herself up for humiliation. If she waited

out back and Joe didn't show, she'd be mortified. Joe's reasons why they shouldn't fraternize made sense, and deep down she couldn't help agreeing with them…but she just couldn't fight the attraction anymore, and if he stood her up she'd be so furious and embarrassed she'd hitchhike out of town—even this late at night—all the way back to San Francisco. And maybe put a hit out on Joe.

Just kidding. Maybe.

Hauling in a deep breath, she barged through the back door. The big spotlight above the door shone over a deserted yard. The pit of her stomach gave way. Then two piercing lights flashed on and off—headlights from a vehicle parked across the entrance to the yard. Joe's pickup truck.

Her rib cage drew tight, and her heart began to pummel. She scampered across the concrete and jumped into the passenger seat, panting as though she'd just held up a bank. Joe faced her, teeth gleaming white in the dimness.

"Evening, sweet pea."

Okay, no hit man required. But this could still be a disaster.

He put the truck into gear and pulled off. For a minute or so they didn't speak, though the silence between them pulsated with surging pheromones and unsteady breathing.

Finally the tension got to be too much for Nina. "Did anyone see you leave?"

"Lots of people saw me leave, but I doubt they suspect anything. You and I seemed to have a convincing argument at the bar. Vince even muttered something to me about easing up on you."

"Oh."

"Just so you know, I have no intention of easing up on

you." He took one of her hands and raised it to his lips. "Especially not tonight."

The promise in his voice sent anticipation streaking through her. She stroked her fingers over his jaw, relishing the prickle of his stubble, looking forward to feeling its rasp against her naked body. He changed his grip on her hand and eased the tip of her middle finger into his mouth. She caught her breath. The suck of his hot, moist mouth tugged at her stomach, unleashing a wave of heat.

"Oh, God." She couldn't deny the naked hunger in her voice.

Joe slowed the truck. They were a few miles out of town, she had no clue where. The headlights picked out a narrow road, trees, fences. Still holding her hand, he guided it to his thigh. Beneath his pants, the muscled heft of his thighs hinted at the virility about to unleash. Her mouth watered.

She squeezed his leg. "So what position do you play?"

"You mean soccer? Center midfielder." He reached over and clasped her thigh. "In bed, I'm up for any position."

His big, confident grasp on her leg made her laugh breathy. "I-I don't know why I asked. I don't have a clue about soccer."

His eyes grew hot. "Don't worry. I'll teach you." He wasn't talking about soccer, she was sure. His hand shifted down to the hem of her plaid skirt. "You changed for me? I'm honored."

"I didn't want to smell like fries and beer."

"Men like fries and beer." He reached the bare flesh above her knee and slipped his hand under her skirt. "I like this even better."

His husky murmur coupled with his sure touch had her

blood pumping. The truck bumped slowly over a rough section of road. She clung onto the armrest, transfixed as Joe stroked her inner thigh, his fingers creating a trail of pleasure across her skin. Her breath came out in fervid puffs. She pressed her booted feet against the floor of the cab, tense with excitement as she silently willed Joe's fingers to move higher and discover the wet craving between her thighs. But each time he extended his reach, his fingers stopped short of her panties, tantalizing her, provoking and intensifying her need.

"Joe," she finally gasped out, writhing against his hand. "You—you're driving me crazy."

He'd slowed the truck until they were inching along.

"Sweet pea, I've been going crazy myself thinking of all the things I want to do with you. And believe me, making you come in my truck while I'm driving is right up there on my list, but I like to do things in the right order. My first priority is to get you into my bedroom, where I'm going to take off your clothes one piece at a time, and then I'm going to kiss you all over and get to know every inch of you before we even think about orgasmic penetration."

His words, uttered in that sexy timbre of his, almost sent her over the edge. Perspiration prickled in her cleavage, her breasts feeling heavy and straining against her bra. What was it about Joe that worked her into such a frenzy? She'd never considered herself sexually aggressive, but now she was ready to tear the clothes off him. Before she could think, she'd moved her hand from his thigh to cup his groin. The heat and size of his bulge dried her throat. He hissed at her, surprise flashing in his chocolate eyes.

"And this?" she asked. "Is this anywhere on your list?"

She kneaded her palm back and forth across his swollen crotch, excited by his reaction.

The truck jerked and bunny hopped. Groaning, Joe grabbed her hand and forced it away. "Christ almighty, if you don't stop now, I'm going to tie you up."

She laughed from sheer exhilaration. Tie her up? Joe was giving her wicked ideas. "I'll behave, as long as we get to your place quick."

"We're almost there."

He swung the wheel and stepped on the accelerator. The truck roared down a long driveway, headlights bouncing off trees and grass before the glare picked out a long, ranch-style house with a wide veranda.

Joe brought the truck to an abrupt halt. They got out, and Joe grabbed her hand and led her into the house. As he flicked on a few lights, she saw a large sitting room with a stone fireplace and raked ceilings.

"So, this is where you live." The comfy armchairs, rugs, and rustic bric-a-brac gave the room a homely atmosphere. Joe's house looked like a cozy, unpretentious place where a person could relax. "Have you been here long?"

"About three years. I'll give you the guided tour later. Right now, there's only one room I want to show you."

Joe swung her into his arms and strode down the hallway. He kicked open a door, walked in, and set her slowly to her feet.

His bedroom. The lights were off, but through the window, faint moonlight spilled across the king-size bed that dominated the room. In the silence, Joe's breathing sounded deep and uneven.

"Joe." She pressed a hand to his chest. "This...this is just for fun, right?" Before they went any further, she needed to know they still agreed on this.

"Of course," he murmured. "No fuss, just pure fun."

He reached for her, and the night swelled and soared around her.

Chapter Six

Nina heard the little gasping noises escaping her lips. A small part of her marveled at how shameless she sounded, but most of her was too high on the pleasure of Joe's mouth on her to notice. He branded sizzling-hot kisses over her throat, ears, and cheeks before moving back to her lips. Lust unfurled in her as she twined her arms around his neck and returned his kisses, leaving nothing in reserve, showing him just how turned on she was.

As his tongue penetrated past her lips, the heat engulfing her arrowed straight for her center, and she wrapped one leg around him, eager to get closer to him. Pushing his hand under her skirt, Joe pulled her thigh tight around him and ground his hips against hers, the hard hump in his trousers fitting perfectly into the apex of her legs. Darkness swirled about her, heady with the scent of their musk. She ran her hands down his back and began to tug his shirt from his pants.

Joe's shoulders bunched up as his fingers got busy with her shirt. It had a tight fit and a long row of buttons.

"Don't want to tear your shirt," he said as he wrestled with the buttons.

Oh, that was sweet of him, trying to preserve her cheap shirt because he was under the impression she was poor. Her breasts ached for his touch, but she waited until he was done. Finally he pulled off her shirt along with her jacket and tossed them to the ground. The sight of her black bra made him pause.

"Oh, yeah. I like this." He ran a finger lightly over the lace trim, leaving her flesh burning.

Lava heat pounded in her breasts, gathered in a liquid pool between her legs. "Why are you waiting?" she breathed, legs trembling. "You've seen the goods before."

"I like seeing them wrapped up in a pretty package."

His eyes feasted on her as he drew his fingers over one bra cup and rested them against the peak. The way Joe ogled her breasts made her feel like a centerfold model. He curved his hands around her waist, found the zipper of her skirt, and made short work of it. The skirt fell around her feet with a soft *whoosh*.

Eek. Now he could see the plain beige panties she'd been forced to buy. She hadn't minded showing them when they'd jumped off the cliff, but now they were in his bedroom, and she wished she had her usual sexy silk thongs. Suddenly self-conscious, she crossed her hands over the bargain-basement panties.

"Hey, what're you trying to hide?" Joe tugged at her hands, grinning.

"Uh, the general store was fresh out of Victoria's Secret."

She reluctantly allowed him to lift her hands away. "It was either this or great big granny panties."

Joe stared greedily at her panties, and then he brushed his palm over them, making her squirm. He chuckled low in his throat. "I can't believe you're embarrassed over this."

Shoot, she was in danger of giving herself away. Ordinary working-class people didn't get hung up because they weren't wearing expensive lingerie.

"I just want to look my best, Joe."

His eyes flared. "Sweet pea, you could make even granny panties look sexy."

"I'll have to test you out on that," she said, snickering.

He groaned. "You're testing me right now." Taking hold of both her hands, he eased them behind her back and lowered his head to her neck. "And I can't resist..." His lips worked their magic on her, and she became boneless with desire as his wide chest rubbed against hers.

Holding her wrists with one hand, he used his free hand to unfasten her bra and cast it aside. He cupped one breast and lowered his head to the other, his lips closing over her nipple. Taking his time, he sucked and stroked and played until she thought she might pass out with sheer pleasure. Moaning, she pushed her leg between his to get to his pulsing heat, and he responded by pressing his upper thigh hard against her mound. Sexual heat inundated her. Her flesh quivered, rippled, engorged, and before she knew it she was on the edge of a climax. But Joe, seeming to sense this, drew his leg away. She was so jellylike she would have collapsed if he hadn't been holding her.

"Joe," she whispered faintly. "You're testing my limits, too, you know."

His rich chuckle ruffled her hair. "But I haven't kissed you all over yet." He returned his attention to her breasts while his hands nudged inside her panties to knead her tight butt.

It wasn't fair that he still had his clothes on. She tried to tear off his shirt but the darn thing was too stubborn. Eventually Joe laughed at her impatience and pulled it off. Nina gulped in admiration as she ate up the sight of his muscled pectorals.

"You're gorgeous," she said as she coasted her hands across his chest, the dark hairs soft against her palm. She nuzzled his nipples and licked a path over his six-pack, breathing in the heady scent of Joe that was all vigorous, lusty male. As she gorged herself on him, she heard his sharp intake of air before he took charge again and lifted her face up to devour her mouth. Taking charge in the bedroom was his thing, she guessed, and she liked it. A whole lot. Somehow his autocratic behavior didn't rile her—instead, it turned her on. Right up to eleven.

While he was kissing her, he got rid of her panties. Now she was naked except for her cowboy boots. She went to pull them off, but Joe halted her.

"No, keep them on." He traced his hands over her thighs. "You look like a pinup for sexiest cowgirl of the year." His husky drawl had her reaching for him, but he held her off. "Stay there."

His eyes never left hers as he rid himself of his shoes, unbuckled his belt, and shucked off his pants. His boxer briefs stretched taut over an impressive-sized package, and she didn't even pretend to look elsewhere. He stripped them off, and heat saturated the folds between her thighs. *My goodness, he's packing some serious equipment there.*

Then he wrapped her in his arms, exploring and kissing every inch of her just like he'd promised, and soon she didn't know whether she was standing or floating upside down. The haze lifted a little when Joe knelt in front of her, skimming his palms down her legs while his thick black hair nestled against her belly. He nibbled his way down her stomach until he reached the patch of blonde curls covering her mound.

He breathed in deeply, hands cupping her ass, before his tongue snaked between her folds and flickered against her slit. Wet heat drenched her in an instant. She arched her back for more. His lick was measured, erotic, explosive. He controlled her, his lapping first greedy then delicate, always sure, extending her exquisite pleasure to the point of torture. His control grew as her restraint crumbled until she couldn't wait any longer, and she raked her fingers through his hair, urging him on as she sought release.

But he denied her the screaming orgasm she wanted so badly and rose to his feet, his face flushed, his lips wet from her moisture. He leisurely fondled her breast. "My hot little cowgirl."

"Joe, I swear…" She could barely speak.

He smiled, cocky, but damn, how she wanted him.

"Wait."

He turned to rummage in the drawer of his nightstand, leaving her to bite her lip as she stared at his taut backside. The urge to hurl herself at him rose, but, as much as she hated admitting it, she was hooked on his domineering lovemaking.

When he turned back, he had a condom on and a burning look in his eyes. He sat on the edge of the bed. "Come here," he ordered.

She moved toward him, lungs aching with anticipation. When she was within arm's length, he grasped her waist and pushed his knees between hers until she stood above him, her legs straddled over his thighs. She met his searing gaze, and when his hands pressed her down, she knew what he wanted. What she wanted so desperately.

As she bent her knees, the tip of his erection found her entrance. Burning hot and hard, it teased her, parting her slick folds. He paused, holding her still. She was ready to collapse, her leg muscles quivering, but he held her up, his biceps bulging from the strain. He eased an inch into her, his heat and strength arousing her further. Bending her head back, she let out a growl of pure animal need and tried to push herself down on him. But Joe prevented her, still controlling her descent. As he let her down one solid inch at a time, his thickness stretched her, filled her, melted her. After several breathless seconds, he settled her on his lap, sheathed in her flesh to the hilt, breathing hard as he smiled at her.

"You feel so good." He took her mouth in one bruising kiss after another until her head was swimming. She moved against him, hands on his shoulders, arching her back as she sought the sweet friction between them. As she'd come to expect, he took over, using his impressive strength to shift her up and down while he thrust himself slowly and evenly into her.

Tension built in her to fever pitch. She tossed her head, wild for release, seeking the button to unleash the pressure. When Joe took her nipple between his lips, she almost bucked right off him, but his hands held her firm. His teeth riffled against her nipple, his thrust pushed her higher, and suddenly she was an explosion of wet, molten flesh, and stars were falling around her, and someone was moaning out, "Oh, God. Oh, Joe," over and over again.

Joe's grunts filtered through the hot mist. She was vaguely aware of his hands digging into her hips and his mouth nipping her shoulder as he drove hard into her. It could have hurt, but it didn't, her wetness assisting his fierce pounding. He gripped her tight, his body tensed as he growled and spasmed deep inside her for several fiery moments, before his body gradually grew slack.

Sighing deeply, he wiped his forearm across his sweaty brow. "Sweet pea, that was the most incredible ride."

She gulped, shaky and throbbing. "You can say that again," she whispered.

He was still buried deep inside her, and she didn't want to let him go. For a while he scattered kisses over her face and neck again, this time his mouth soft, gentle, reassuring. When he finally lifted her off his lap, the night air nipped at her, raising goose bumps on her bottom. Joe got rid of the condom, pulled off her boots, and held up the quilt covering the bed. "Come here, sweet pea."

She slipped gratefully under the covers, Joe quickly joining her. The sheets were cool, but Joe pulled her into his arms, his warmth surrounding her. She turned to him, surprised and a little dismayed at how eagerly she sought him out. Was it simply because Joe had given her the best sex of her life? Or was there something more to it?

Joe didn't seem to be troubled by such worries. He kissed her hair and wrapped his arms around her. "Just a heads-up. I'm going to let you rest for a little while, but in about ten minutes I have another activity planned for us."

Anticipation stirred in her loins. She shifted her legs against his. "What kind of activity?"

"It's a surprise."

"Can't you give me a clue?"

His lips curled into a lazy, teasing smile. "All I'll tell you is that I'm going to make you say 'Oh, God' and 'Oh, Joe' again. Several times. Maybe if I make the right moves, I'll even get you to scream it out. Sound good to you?"

Nina nodded, her hunger already returning. Whatever Joe did to her would be good, as long as she remembered that this was just sex. Great, awesome sex, yes, but that was all it was. It didn't—couldn't—change anything between them.

• • •

Joe peered down at Nina's prone form. She looked deeply asleep, which was no wonder, considering the epic sex they'd enjoyed through the night. But dawn was touching the bedroom curtains, and he had to rouse her.

Gently he shook her awake. "Hey, sleepyhead. It's time to get up."

"Wha…?" She yawned, blonde hair sexily tousled, lips still swollen from all that kissing.

His cock stirred. If only he could strip again and join her in the bed for an early morning quickie… But that was asking for even more trouble.

Nina blinked several times before her blue eyes cleared and focused on him already dressed in jeans and a T-shirt. "Where're you going?"

"I'm taking you back to the inn before anyone else gets there." He paused before sinking on the bed next to her.

"Nina, last night was incredible, but…"

Her mouth turned down. "But you don't want a repeat?"

"Of course I want a repeat," he answered quickly, even as the logical part of his brain told him that was a dumb idea. Even dumber than last night. But his body was completely enthralled with her. "I want you in my bed as often as possible, but it has to stay between us. I can't have the rest of the staff finding out. Not because I'm ashamed to be with you, but—"

"I understand." She squeezed his hand briefly. "This is just a bit of fun between you and me, right? Nothing serious. We don't need the whole town sticking their noses into our private business."

He breathed out a sigh of relief. Nina understood his dilemma, and she wasn't fussed about keeping this a secret. It wasn't how he usually conducted his brief affairs, but then again he'd never had an affair with an employee. Again, his logical brain sent out a warning, but he ignored it. Nina was in his bloodstream, and for however long this crazy fever lasted, he was her captive.

• • •

Nina yawned as she scraped and rinsed plates. The bustle in the kitchen was dying down after the dinner rush, but she still had plenty of clearing up to do. It didn't help that she'd barely caught a few hours' sleep last night. She closed her eyes, and for a moment she was transported back to the heady sweetness of being with Joe. All day the memories of him had teased her. Tonight he'd gone to his usual soccer practice, which was just as well. She didn't need him distracting her again in front of staff and customers.

"Glad you've got time to daydream." Sarah's bark sounded just inches from her ear.

Nina jerked, and the plate she'd been holding slipped and crashed to the floor. "Oh, crap!"

Sarah's lips thinned as others paused to see the cause of the commotion. "Well, that's one way of doing the dishes. I'll tell Joe to dock your pay again. What's that, like your fourth since you started?"

"Only my third." Nina grabbed a brush and pan and began cleaning up the broken plate. "And I don't mind Joe docking my pay."

"I thought you were desperate for a job." Sarah continued to stand over her, and when Nina straightened, the head chef's face was filled with suspicion. "I already know you lied about working in a coffee shop. And now you're acting like you don't even care about the money you're losing. So why are you really here in Hartley?"

Nina tossed the ceramic shards into the garbage bin, making as much clatter as she could. She'd been too quick to shrug off her docked pay. She should've acted more concerned.

"I'm here to make a fresh start," she said as calmly as possible.

"Yeah?" Sarah didn't seem convinced.

Nina was saved from having to say more by Mrs. Stewart appearing in the kitchen. She and her friend had dined at the restaurant earlier, and when Nina served them, Mrs. Stewart had made some coy remarks about Joe. Now, as the smiling woman advanced on them, Nina prayed she wouldn't say anything embarrassing in front of Sarah.

"That chicken was delicious!" Mrs. Stewart beamed at Sarah. "You must keep that on the menu permanently."

"Thanks, Mrs. Stewart." The head chef grinned. If there was one thing that softened her up, it was compliments on her cooking. "Is there anything else I can get you?"

"No, thank you. I really came back here to talk to Nina."

Sarah's frown returned. "Sure," she replied, but instead of leaving, she stood right there, looking suspicious.

"How can I help you?" Nina asked Mrs. Stewart, hoping she wouldn't mention Joe again.

"It's about the Food and Wine Festival. You know about it, right?"

Nina nodded. She'd seen all the posters around town and knew Joe was on the organizing committee.

"The thrift store will have a stall at the festival," Mrs. Stewart continued. "We're accepting all kinds of donations to sell. My niece usually helps me, but she's broken her leg, poor thing, so I was hoping you'd volunteer."

The festival was in two weeks, and by the end of that weekend, Nina's three-week vacation from Beaumont, Inc. would be over and she'd have to return to San Francisco. The dreaded reminder, coupled with Mrs. Stewart's request, threw Nina into confusion. "Oh, um, yeah, well—"

"Of course she'd love to help you," Sarah broke in with a smirk at Nina. "She wants to make a fresh start in Hartley, and what better way is there than getting involved in our local charity?"

Nina coughed. "Well, sure." She hesitated a second before nodding firmly. She'd still be here for the festival, anyway. "Yes, I'd love to help you, Mrs. Stewart."

"Oh, good! I'm so pleased. I'll talk to you later when

you're not so busy. Good night, dears." She waved a general good-bye before trotting out of the kitchen, leaving Nina and Sarah alone.

"I'm happy to help Mrs. Stewart." Nina stuck her chin out. "She's nice, and she gives people the benefit of the doubt."

Sarah looked down at her. "Just remember to keep your volunteering to your off hours. You're paid to work here."

Nina bit back a quick retort. No point aggravating the head chef.

By the time Nina had finished her kitchen duties, the restaurant was closed, and only a few quiet drinkers were left. Nina looked about the bar expectantly, hoping that Joe had returned from soccer practice, but he was nowhere to be seen, and disappointment pinched her.

"Hey, Nina," Vince called from behind the counter where he was carefully filling a glass from a beer bottle.

She hitched her butt onto a stool at the counter. Even though her shift had ended, she didn't want to go to her bare, lonely room. Not when a part of her was still hoping for Joe to return, even though he'd never made any promises.

"What's that?" she asked, glad for the distraction from Joe. She nodded at the unlabeled bottle from which a rich, golden-brown beer flowed steadily into the glass.

"It's an IPA from a local microbrewery," Vince said.

"IPA?"

"India pale ale." He grinned. "Clearly you're not into beer."

"Sorry, no."

He slid the glass to her. "Try it. You might like it."

Shrugging, she took a cautious sip and rolled the liquid

around her mouth before swallowing. "Hey, that's not your normal beer. It's kind of chewy and bitey."

"Hoppy, you mean."

"If you say so. It's really good. Where did you get it from?"

"The shed in my backyard." Vince retrieved the glass and took a satisfying swallow. "It's a hobby of mine, brewing beer."

Nina sat up. "You have a brewery? Do you sell your beer here?"

He shook his head, wiping the back of his hand across his mouth. "Nah. Joe doesn't know about it."

"But you're friends. How does he not know?"

"Well, he knows I brew beer, but he doesn't know I've upgraded my equipment to commercial grade." A diffident expression came over Vince's face. "I've been meaning to ask him if I can stock some of it here, but, well, he has enough on his plate at the moment, what with his bank problems and those Beaumont shitheads who want his property and…"

Nina's heart stopped for several seconds as Vince continued to talk. *What did he just say? Those Beaumont shitheads? He can't mean—*

"Hey, Joe." Vince's words broke through her whirling thoughts, and her heart stuttered to life, suddenly pounding like a runaway freight train.

"Hey, Vince. Hi, Nina."

Joe stood right behind her. Every nerve ending in her body shrieked out his presence as she turned to face him.

"Hi." She sounded like a frightened mouse.

She tried to take a breath, but it was difficult with Joe so close to her. He was freshly showered after his soccer game, his body giving off waves of clean masculinity that pulled her in. His warm, expressive gaze traveled over her like he'd missed her, but then, as if becoming aware that Vince was still there, he glanced away, and she was able to breathe.

Joe talked to Vince, but she barely listened as Vince's words whirred in her mind. Beaumont shitheads. *Beaumont.* What exactly did he mean by that? Was there some connection between Joe and her dad? *Unlikely*, she told herself. Beaumont was a common enough surname. And why would a billionaire like her dad be interested in a small place like the Comet Inn? It didn't make sense. Vince must have meant someone else.

"Penny for your thoughts?" Joe said.

She came to with a start. The bar was emptying, and Vince had begun closing up. She was alone with Joe. He rested one elbow on the counter, and although his stance was casual, the look in his eye was anything but.

She swallowed, deciding to set aside her concerns about what Vince had said. It was much nicer to concentrate on Joe. "Just one penny? Is that all my thoughts are worth?"

He glanced quickly about, then angled his body so that no one but she could see his face. "That depends. If you're thinking what I'm thinking, then I'd be willing to pay you more."

She sucked her lower lip, wondering what he was thinking. From last night she knew Joe had some pretty dirty thoughts.

He uttered a groan so soft only she could hear it. "Don't do that with your lip. Unless you want me sporting wood in public."

She sputtered with laughter. Only Joe could get her so

excited with so little. Before she could respond, Vince came back behind the counter and shot a weird look at her. Afraid he would recognize the lust in her face, she pushed to her feet.

"I'm exhausted. I'm going to bed. Good night, all." She made a general wave to encompass both Joe and Vince before beating a hasty retreat.

If Joe wanted a repeat of last night, then he'd have to come and get her, she decided as she made her way to her room. Even if she couldn't stop thinking about him, she didn't want to appear too eager. Taking a shower didn't stop her thinking of him, either. In fact, it made it worse. By the time she returned to her room, she was wondering how she'd ever get to sleep.

She let out a shriek as she spotted Joe lying fully clothed on her bed. "Oh, sweet Jesus, you scared me! Why didn't you warn me?"

He heaved himself up to a sitting position. "Do you always walk around in nothing but a towel after your shower? I'll have to buy you a bathrobe."

Excitement shivered through her. She walked up to him until they were almost touching. "Why?" She licked her lips. "Are you planning to surprise me in my room on a regular basis?"

He reached up and placed his hands on her hips, his fingers anchoring her towel. "That depends."

"On what?"

"On whether you give me what I want." His grip on her towel firmed. She swayed and allowed the towel to slip away until it crumpled to the floor. Joe's hands remained on her hips, his expression almost reverential as he took in her nakedness. "Oh, sweet pea," he breathed. "You're perfect."

She was far from perfect, but Joe's reaction filled her with a strange, heady sensation. What if she was perfect *for him*? Heat swept over her, plumping her breasts, making her nipples harden. Joe cupped a hand to her breast, fingers teasing her nipple even harder.

"Yes, perfect." He stared up at her with hunger stamped across his face.

Her knees buckled as she slid onto his lap, straddling his denim-clad thighs. She speared her fingers through his hair, and then their mouths met and fused with desire. They kissed frantically, his fingers imprinted into her back, she pressing herself into him, desperate for contact.

"Wait," she panted when she was forced to come up for air. "What about Vince?"

"Damn." He gave her ass a soft pinch. "I'm sure as hell not sharing you with Vince."

Ooh, I like that, she thought in surprise. She liked Joe pinching her ass. She let out a mock growl. "I meant is there any chance he might've seen you come into my room?"

"No. He's gone home, and I locked up the inn." His thumb absently stroked her butt cheek where he'd pinched her. "There're only two guests upstairs. So it's just you and me, sweet pea."

Every time he called her sweet pea it sent a thrill straight to her heart. She brushed her lips teasingly against his. "That's good. Why didn't you take off your clothes while you were waiting for me?"

"I didn't want to be presumptuous." His eyes glinted as his hand wandered around her ass. He began stroking between her thighs.

Her breathing stalled as his fingers caressed her, sweeping from front to back, exploring every inch of her. She didn't have time to be embarrassed at how thoroughly he was touching her; she was too caught up in the magic of his fingers. Blood thudded in her veins, desire coiled in her center, tension winding her up tighter and higher.

"You're so wet," Joe murmured, his eyes on fire.

Suddenly she was mad for him, mad to feel him inside her. She grabbed at his belt buckle. "Get this off." She growled in frustration. "Quick. Now."

"But you're so close." His fingers circled her entrance, and she shuddered, almost climaxing but holding herself back.

"I want you in me." She practically snarled, tugging his belt free.

Joe's eyes widened. "Yes, ma'am."

He grabbed a condom from his pocket. Then, with her help, he unzipped his jeans and shoved them and his boxers down to his knees. He had barely sheathed himself before Nina leaped back onto his lap, positioning herself over his rigid erection. He didn't wait. Grabbing her by the hips, he drove her down onto him without finesse, with just plain, raw sexual need. And that excited her more than she'd anticipated. Joe was in her, around her. He filled her up and surrounded her until there was nothing in her world but him.

He rolled her onto her back and shifted the angle of his body so he could thrust even harder into her. She felt herself spiraling up, caught in the sensations of his body pumping into hers. And then his mouth found hers again, and he was kissing her like he could never sate his appetite. His fingers found her aching nipple, and his other hand slid between their heaving bodies and pressed against her clit.

All erogenous zones on fire, she gripped her knees against him and came in a roaring climax that shook her to her hair roots, so she was only barely aware when, short seconds later, Joe erupted inside her. He let out a long, deep groan before collapsing onto her. He lay there panting for a moment then rolled off her, wrapping his arms around her so that she lay half on top of him.

"Yeah, perfect," he said as he planted a clumsy kiss on her hair.

Nina didn't say anything as she curled closer to him. Yes, sex with Joe was perfect. It was just everything else that was not so perfect.

Chapter Seven

As Nina approached Joe's office, she couldn't stop her imagination from running wild. Had Joe summoned her there just so he could kiss her, even though it was Friday at noon and the inn was bustling with preparations for the busy weekend? But her anticipation died as soon as she stepped inside and saw Joe sitting behind the desk squinting at his laptop.

His smile of greeting was warm, but he waved her to the chair on the opposite side of the desk. Clearly he hadn't called her in for a make-out session. Too bad.

"Your pay." He slid a check with an attached paystub across the desk toward her.

"Oh." It felt wrong to accept money from Joe. He worked so hard for it, while she had millions of dollars doing nothing in her bank account. But, she reminded herself, she had come here to prove to herself that she could survive without her trust fund or her name. She was entitled to her wages.

She inspected the figures on the paycheck and frowned.

"You forgot to deduct the breakages."

He shrugged. "Everyone breaks a few things when they first start."

"But you don't sleep with every new employee."

"What's your point?"

"My point is I don't want any special treatment. For whatever reason."

They stared at each other for a beat before Joe sighed. "Fine." He took the paycheck from her.

"And don't forget the forty dollars you loaned me."

He wrote out a new check and handed it to her. "Happy now?"

"Yup." She smiled at the meager figure on the check.

Joe grinned back at her, and as always, his smile infected her with happiness. But the moment was broken as a sharp gust of wind blew in from the open window. Joe got up and walked to the window, his expression suddenly somber.

Outside, storm clouds were rolling in, black with thunderous intent, and in just a few seconds the room had noticeably darkened.

"Damn, I was hoping we'd miss this storm." Joe scanned the leaden sky. "But it looks like we're going to get hammered."

He'd barely spoken before a fork of lightning lit up the sky, and they both flinched. Thunder was quick to follow, rumbling ominously; the storm was closing in fast on Hartley.

"Shit. I have to go." Joe turned to Nina, his brow creased with concern. "This storm might tear my place apart."

"Your place? But your house seems solid enough."

"Not my house, my…" He blinked at her as if he'd only just realized what he was saying. "My other investment property. It's run-down, and I don't know how it'll hold up against this storm." He grabbed the jacket slung over his desk chair, and strode toward the door.

His concerned expression made her worried on his behalf. "Wait for me." Nina hurried after him. "I can help you."

Joe hesitated in midstride. "You?"

"Yes, me. I've finished my morning chores. Just give me a second to get a sweater or something and I'll go with you."

He scratched his chin, but then another flash of lightning appeared to make up his mind. He nodded. "Make it quick."

Nina dashed next door to her room, where she tucked away her paycheck and grabbed the gray hoodie she'd bought from the thrift store. Joe was waiting for her in the reception lobby. He tossed a yellow rain slicker at her and jerked his head in the direction of the door.

"Let's go."

The air was thick and heavy as they drove out of Hartley in Joe's truck. Dark clouds curdled overhead, but the rain held off for the moment. The road seemed familiar. They were heading toward the cliffs where Joe had brought her earlier that week—had it only been on Monday? But then he took a different turn down a narrow, rutted lane.

Five minutes later they pulled up outside a rambling old house surrounded by several acres of weed-infested land. Despite its neglected air, the house was still grand and gracious. Its stone walls were weathered to the color of honey, and in the dilapidated grounds were traces of a once manicured lawn. The best feature of the property was its location, situated on a rise overlooking the ocean, with stands of red oaks surrounding it. Oaks that were buffeted by the rising winds.

As they hurried to the house, gusts of wind heralded the arrival of the storm, and a few seconds later the clouds dumped rain in giant bucketfuls. The interior of the house was cavernous and gloomy. Nina had a brief impression of soaring ceilings, arched windows, and carved timber. And over that, peeling paint, moldy walls, and rotting decay.

Joe had brought some folded-up tarpaulins with him. He started for the once magnificent staircase. "Follow me."

The rat-a-tat of the rain grew louder as they dashed upward, and the stairs became narrower as they ascended to the third floor, where the attics crouched just beneath the roof. A door banged in the rising wind. Joe stepped into the closest attic and swore under his breath.

"Look at that."

The window to the attic had blown out, leaving a gaping hole through which rain poured inside. The roof had sprung several leaks, some of them drips, others almost rivers. The wind howled and flurried about the house, rattling every nail, shaking every timber.

Joe made a quick survey of the other two attics, Nina close behind him. Both of them had also sprung copious leaks.

"Let's fix that blown-out window first," Joe said, throwing down his pile of tarpaulins.

Nina helped as best she could, following his instructions and trying to ignore the rain slapping at her. She'd never experienced anything like this before, and soon she was soaked and freezing, despite the rain slicker. But she didn't allow herself to complain. How could she when Joe was working even harder than she was?

Together they fastened a tarpaulin over the broken window, which required Joe to hang out dangerously from the ledge. They rigged up other tarpaulins beneath the worst of the leaks so that the water was diverted outside the house. Smaller leaks were dealt with using the pails and cans that had obviously been put to the same use before.

The violent storm passed as quickly as it came, leaving behind a sodden, dripping house. They trudged downstairs to the first floor, where a few more windows were broken and water pooled in several places.

"What made you buy this place?" Nina asked, unable to contain her curiosity any longer.

Joe swiped a hand across his damp brow as he glanced around the reception room they stood in. "I've always admired this house. As soon as it came up for sale, I had to buy it. It's a wreck now, but it's got great potential. I want to turn it into a high-end boutique B&B. Hartley's becoming more popular, and an upmarket B&B will fill a gap."

"It's definitely got loads of character."

Something about the house reminded her of the faded mansion she'd grown up in. Her mom had adored grand old houses, and her dad had indulged her. Nina had fond memories of sliding down banisters and running through half-finished rooms. Then her mom had died, and when her dad had remarried, her stepmom had turned her childhood home into a mini Palace of Versailles.

Nina flicked a piece of peeling wallpaper. "But you'll need a lot of money to turn this into a B&B."

"Tell me something I don't know."

The odd note in his voice made her frown as a memory triggered. What had Vince said about Joe's bank problems?

"Are you having trouble getting a loan?" she asked before she could stop herself.

His eyes sharpened on her. "Who told you that?"

"Uh, no one. Just a guess."

Uneasiness rolled in her stomach. Money. Always rearing its ugly head. Joe wasn't like her jerk of an ex, though, was he? He wouldn't ask her for money. But what if he found out how wealthy she was? Would that make a difference?

Joe riffled his fingers through his hair as he gazed out a missing window at the storm-churned sea. "Well, it's true," he said reluctantly. "But that's not the half of it."

"There's more?"

"Yup. Someone's trying to make me sell this place."

The uneasiness in her stomach congealed into cold dread. "Who?" she forced herself to ask, sensing she wouldn't like the answer.

"A billionaire bastard named Carson Beaumont. Ever heard of him?"

Thank God he had his back to her or he surely would have noticed her shock. She felt the blood draining from her cheeks, leaving her shaky and weak.

"Uh, n-no, don't think so." What else could she say? She hated lying about such an important fact, especially after she'd promised him no more lies, but what choice did she have when he'd just labeled her father a bastard?

"You're lucky, then." Joe was still staring out the window. "Beaumont wants this property because of the sea views and because it's the only access to a huge plot of land farther back where he wants to build another of his obscene megaresorts. He's already made me several offers. Oh, not him personally, of course. He sends up his goons to do his dirty work."

"Dirty work?" She felt as hollow as she sounded.

"Yeah. I think they've been whispering to the banks, discouraging them from giving me a loan." His hands curled into fists, and his shoulders grew rigid. "And they know my grandmother is in a nursing home. They know to the dollar how much it costs me each month, so they're trying to use that as leverage on me." Veins bulged in his hands. "Fuckers."

Nina sucked in tiny sips of air as her ribs threatened to crush her lungs. "That's vile," she choked out.

God, this was so much worse than she could have imagined. How dare her father treat Joe—or anyone—like this? It was contemptible, immoral. Were Beaumont, Inc.'s managers acting on their own or only carrying out orders? It didn't really matter. Her father had always been a ruthless businessman. He pressed his subordinates to get results, no matter what. He was responsible.

What could she do about it, though? Should she call her dad and demand he back off from Joe? But he wouldn't, because he'd never taken her seriously and she wasn't the apple of his eye like Brooke was. He wouldn't because business always came first. He wouldn't because *she* never came first with him. What she wanted and what she cared about didn't matter to him.

"Hey, what's wrong?"

Joe's soft query came from closer than she'd expected, and she saw that he was right in front of her, eyes dark with concern.

She folded her arms around herself, feeling sick and cold. "I wish I could help you."

"You have helped me, just now." His mouth lifted in a small smile. "Thank you, Nina."

His thanks only made her feel worse. She didn't deserve

his thanks. She was the enemy because of her name.

"I didn't expect such a bad storm. I've been trying to find the time to weatherize this place before winter comes," Joe continued. "Guess I should get a move on it now."

"Let me help you," she said, consumed by guilt. "When I'm free, of course. I won't neglect my duties at the inn."

He seemed surprised but pleased. "That'd be great, thanks. I'll see if I can get some of my buddies to help over the weekend, too."

He shifted toward her, his hands gripping her elbows. He wanted to uncross her arms, she intuited, and by the look in his eyes, he wanted to kiss her. But this time, her desire was no match for a guilty conscience, and she kept her arms firmly locked.

A frown touched Joe's brow, and some of the warmth ebbed from his eyes. Instead of embracing her, he brushed her cheek briefly. "You must be freezing. Let's get back to the inn."

She followed him out, her heart as heavy as the clouds hanging overhead.

• • •

Work was a welcome distraction from a troubled conscience. The inn was full that weekend, and Sarah was short in the kitchen again. Nina didn't mind being the target of Sarah's quick temper. She preferred being busy to dwelling on Joe's problems with Beaumont, Inc. and how she was concealing her identity from him. When her shift on Friday night ended, Joe told her to get a good night's rest and he'd see her in the morning. She was almost relieved not to spend the night with him, but in the small hours of the morning she woke up cold and lonely and missing the heat of his body.

Saturday was hectic, too. After finishing her morning chores, she discovered that Vince was preparing to go and help Joe weatherize his B&B mansion, and immediately she insisted on going with him. At the house were three men, all friends of Joe's. Joe was apparently up on the roof. The men eyed her curiously when Vince introduced her but soon turned their attention back to work.

Nina was doing her best to caulk a leaky window when Joe walked up to her.

"Hey, you're here," he said, surprise and pleasure on his face.

As always, her heart flipped at his appearance. "I said I would be."

"You didn't have to, you know."

But she did, she really did—to make up for her dad causing him trouble, however small the gesture. The more she got to know Joe, the more she admired him. He didn't deserve to be bullied into selling his dream. She wanted to help him succeed in any way she could.

"I know I don't have to; I want to. But I'm not exactly the world's best handyman." She gave a wry nod at the smeary line of filler she'd laid down.

"Here, let me teach you." Before she could blink, Joe had wrapped his hand around hers holding the caulking gun. There was no one else in the room. He leaned into her, his breath feathering her cheek. "See, you just need a steady hand…"

Their bodies melded together. His groin nestled against her ass. His hand wasn't so steady, and neither was her heart.

"Joe…someone might come in."

Reluctantly, he let her go. "Maybe we can meet tonight?" His voice was thick with need.

She nodded, her blood fevered. But before she could say anything, Joe's friend Paul walked into the room, Joe stepped away from her, and the moment was over.

With a sigh, Nina returned to her task. She hadn't been at it five minutes before her cell phone rang.

"Hey, girlfriend," Lindsey chirped in her ear. "Thought I'd better check on you, since I haven't heard from you in more than a week."

"Oh, hi, Lindsey." Nina paused to check the room was empty. She didn't need anyone overhearing her conversation. "Sorry I haven't called earlier. Things have been…hectic." That was one way of putting it.

"Glad to hear you're still alive, at least. Can you tell me where you're staying in case I need to get a hold of you?"

"Sure. I'm at the Comet Inn in Hartley."

"Uh-huh. So how's the whole incognito thing going?"

"It's been…interesting."

"Oh, yeah? Whatcha doing right now?"

Nina held up a caulk-spattered hand and chuckled. "You'd never guess. I'm covered in grime, I look awful, and I have hours of work ahead of me, but somehow I'm enjoying myself."

"Hmm. You sound different. More relaxed and carefree." Lindsey paused. "So. What's his name?"

Nina spluttered. "His name?"

"The name of the guy who's made you so relaxed and carefree."

Nina rolled her eyes. Lindsey knew her too well. "His

name is Joe. And it's not what you think."

"I'll bet. It's probably worse." Lindsey chuckled. "Have fun, darling. Just don't get too involved. Remember you're returning to San Francisco in two weeks."

Nina sighed. "I won't forget." But she had managed to push that inconvenient fact to the back of her mind.

"I'll leave you to your fun with Joe. Just be careful, okay?"

"Yes, *Mom*. Thanks for calling."

Lindsey's advice was sound, but how could she be careful around Joe when all he had to do was walk into a room to get her hormones jumping? She'd practically swooned when he'd suggested they might meet that night, and as the afternoon wore on, she found herself praying her hopes would come true.

To make matters worse, it was such a struggle pretending there was nothing going on between them when she was microscopically aware of his presence. Each time he came close to her, her entire body fluttered with anticipation, and just the sound of his voice in another room was enough to make her prickle with pleasure.

She wasn't being honest with him about her identity, but there was nothing fake about her body's reaction to him. She wanted to be with him, desperately. She wanted another blissful night with him, where hot, earthy sex would make everything else inconsequential. Where she could forget who she was, where she came from, everything. She wanted to lose herself with Joe.

But Saturday night she fell asleep on her own, again.

After several hours at Joe's B&B, she and Vince returned to the inn to prepare for the evening rush. Joe stayed behind and didn't come back, even when dinner was in full swing. She overheard Sarah asking Vince if he knew where Joe was, and Vince had replied that Joe was still at the B&B and wasn't expected back.

Nina went to bed wondering if she'd ever spend another night with him.

• • •

Joe shifted in his seat as he tried to stay awake while Nonna Lina rambled on about the dog she'd owned when she was a little girl. He never missed his visits to his nonna, and his Sunday visits were longer. He could've used a morning to sleep in after his long day on Saturday, but he was up bright and early at the inn to make sure guests were checked out properly and handle any possible complaints. Then he'd gone back to weatherizing his B&B before it was time for his soccer match. He'd almost decided to skip soccer until he realized they had no substitutes, his team was almost in the semifinals, and he couldn't let them down at the crucial moment. He'd have to return to his B&B after his visiting Nonna, but for now he should give her his full attention.

"What was his name again?" Nonna Lina's brow puckered up with the effort of remembering. "Was it Lucky? Or Patch? Oh, dear. I'm getting too old."

"Your dog's name was Sampson." Joe had heard about her dog countless times before. He patted her hand. "And you're not too old. You've got years and years left ahead of you."

She gave him a fond smile. "You always cheer me up, Joe. You're a good boy."

But as Joe left a half hour later, his heart was heavy. What would happen if he could no longer afford the fees of the nursing home? What if he couldn't get his bank loan, and the mortgage repayments on the potential B&B slowly bled him dry? In that scenario, he would sell the property to Beaumont, of course. No contest there, not with his nonna's well-being in the balance. But his soul flinched at the thought of caving to Beaumont, of losing his dream and saddling the town with a resort most locals didn't want.

He had to stay positive, he told himself, and get his property weatherproof so he wouldn't have to spend even more money on it.

When he reached his B&B, he was surprised to see Vince and Paul's trucks already parked there. But inside, the first person he bumped into was Nina.

She beamed at him. "Hey, boss."

"Nina? I didn't expect to see you here." His spirits lifted. Her hair was disheveled, her clothes were crumpled, and her garish turquoise Crocs were dull with dust. And she'd never looked more ravishing. "Actually, I didn't expect to see *anyone* here again today."

"Nina roped us in," Vince said as he clomped down the stairs with Paul, a stepladder balanced between them.

"She said she'd buy us each a case of beer," Paul added, winking at Nina.

"A case!" She chuckled. "Liar. It was one beer each."

"One beer." Paul sighed as he shook his head. "You're lucky I'm a sucker for a pretty face."

They all laughed, but Joe felt a tightening in the tendons of his neck. Paul was one of his closest friends, but damn if he didn't feel a twinge of jealousy at his blatant flirting with

Nina.

"Beers are on me," Joe said loudly. "When we're done."

"Shouldn't take long," Paul said. "We're going to seal up some of the shutters." The two men trooped out with their stepladder, leaving Joe alone with Nina.

"Thanks," he said, rubbing the back of his neck. He wasn't used to feeling grateful to her.

She shrugged, looked just as discomfited as him. "It was nothing. I knew you were busy with soccer and your grand-mother today, and you're worried about the weather, so I was hoping to spare you some hassle…"

Nina rattled on like she was nervous about something. But what? He'd caught her giving him some strange looks ever since she'd found out about this B&B, but he couldn't figure out the reason. Maybe she was worried he'd made a bad investment.

"Thank you," he said quietly. "I really appreciate it."

She wriggled her foot, still looking a little jumpy. "You're welcome."

Her soft voice pierced him with longing, and he wished they were alone so he could kiss her nose. Or, better still, he wished they didn't have to pretend they were nothing to each other. He wished they could touch each other in public and not give a damn about onlookers. Well, he could hardly complain, since he'd made the rules. Only, sometimes, he wasn't so sure about the reasons for those rules anymore.

On impulse, he stepped right into her personal space and cupped his hands around her face. She blinked up at him in surprise, her cheeks cool and creamy beneath his rough palms. Her eyes were deep aquamarine as she quivered in his hold, and once again he wondered about the cause behind her tension. Then he dropped his mouth onto hers, a brief, starving kiss that didn't satisfy, only whetted his appetite. But that was all he could allow himself right now.

"I'd better go check up on those two," he said gruffly, "seeing as I promised them beer."

Chapter Eight

"Got any plans for today?" Joe's eyes gleamed at Nina, indicating he definitely had a plan or two. The last of the weekend guests had just checked out, meaning Nina had no more duties at the inn that day.

Nina grinned, trying and not succeeding to tamp down the fluttery feelings he always triggered in her. Honestly, her feelings for Joe were beginning to verge on serious, which was kind of scary.

"Why?" She couldn't stop herself batting her eyelashes at him. "What do you have in mind?"

"I thought I could make it up to you for being so preoccupied these past couple days." His admiring gaze slipped over her, lingering on her breasts. "I was going to start that last night, but it didn't turn out that way."

She understood. Last night at the bar, Paul had drunk too much and got mushy about some girl who'd dumped him. Joe had had to drive him home.

"How is Paul?" she asked.

Joe lifted a shoulder. "I called him this morning. He's hungover, but he'll survive." He leaned closer. "But I don't want to talk about Paul. What are *you* doing today?"

The hunger in his eyes made her sigh. When Joe wanted something, he was irresistible. "I'm helping Mrs. Stewart with her charity stall this morning, but I should be free after that."

His eyebrows shot up. "You're helping Mrs. Stewart?"

"Yeah." She put a hand on her hip. "Why are you so surprised?"

"I guess I wasn't expecting it."

Feeling awkward, she huffed out a breath. "Well, I want to. Okay?"

"Okay." Joe chuckled. "I'll pick you up here around three, then."

"You seem very sure that I want to be picked up."

Leaning in, he traced a finger along the line of her jaw, sending a quiver of pleasure through her. "Yes, sweet pea, I'm very sure about what you want." He ghosted his mouth over hers, hot with promise, but only for a second before he stepped back.

"Don't be late."

And damn if he didn't pat her ass as he walked off.

• • •

Donations for the charity stall had been coming in for days. Nina, Mrs. Stewart, and Patty Williams, another volunteer, set to work combing through them for any quality pieces they could sell at the festival.

"People donate stuff like this?" Nina wrinkled her nose at a moth-eaten coat she pulled out of a black garbage bag. "No one will want this."

"Don't be so hasty," Mrs. Stewart said. "It's not good enough for the festival, but we'll put it in the dollar bargain box here in the store. Winter's coming, and some folks around here can't be too choosy."

Nina instantly felt bad. What did she know about real poverty? "You're right, and I should know better." She folded the coat and placed it in the box for the thrift store.

"No, it's good you haven't reached that level." Mrs. Stewart smiled at her. "You seem to be settling in. Everything okay at the Comet Inn?"

Nina nodded. "I'm still breaking dishes, but I'm getting better."

"Joe's a good boss to have. And a good friend, too." Mrs. Stewart paused, and Nina knew she was thinking about last week when she'd seen Nina and Joe together on the balcony.

"Yeah, Joe's nice," Nina replied, keeping a straight face.

She delved into the next garbage bag. Expecting another bunch of ratty clothing, she wasn't prepared for what she found.

"Hey, Mrs. Stewart, look at these." She held up several dresses, all of them simply designed in muted shades of taupe, mushroom, and ivory.

Mrs. Stewart gave them a cursory glance. "They look nice."

Patty squinted at the dresses. "I dunno. They seem a bit dull to me."

"But they're Favreau." Nina didn't need to check the labels to know these were the same chic, expensive French-designed dresses that her high-society stepmother favored.

Favreau wasn't as instantly recognizable as other big French designers, but wealthy people like Ellen preferred the exclusivity. "They're made in France. These dresses should definitely be in the charity stall."

"Are you sure?" Patty eyed the dresses doubtfully.

"Yes!" Nina nodded eagerly. "Price them at fifty dollars, and they'd be gone in a flash. In fact, you could probably sell them for sixty, seventy dollars. Each of these dresses would retail for several thousand dollars." She scrambled through the bag and pulled out more clothing. "Look, there are pants and jackets, too. You could make a fortune here."

Mrs. Stewart and Patty both stared at her.

"I've never heard of this Favreau." Patty sounded accusing. "You seem to know a lot about French clothes."

Nina halted, belatedly realizing her faux pas. Mrs. Stewart also appeared confused. Okay…she'd slipped up again. An ordinary working-class girl like she was meant to be might know about Christian Dior and Valentino, but she shouldn't recognize a niche brand like Favreau.

"Um, I used to do some babysitting for a rich woman in San Francisco," she quickly improvised. "She wore dresses like these. That's how I know."

"I see." But Patty still seemed a little suspicious. "It's just that you knew what they were so quickly. You didn't even read the labels."

Nina shrugged. "I guess I have an eye for detail, that's all." She turned to Mrs. Stewart. "So, should I price them and put them aside for the festival stall?"

"Maybe just a few." Mrs. Stewart was still doubtful. "And definitely don't price anything above thirty dollars. We don't want to end up with a lot of unsold stock."

Thirty dollars! They might as well give them away. But Nina held her tongue, afraid she'd blow her cover, and did as she was told.

At lunchtime they stopped for coffee and a quick sandwich. Patty seemed to have gotten over her doubts about Nina, as she chatted to her about her family and her occupations. She was on the festival organizing committee, it turned out, and was another fan of Joe's. Under Joe's leadership, the festival had grown each year and was now a great tourist attraction.

"We pride ourselves on our individuality and craftsmanship," Patty said, sounding like a brochure. "People visit here because they like a personal touch. That's why we're so opposed to having a Beaumont resort foisted upon us."

Nina's heart sank at the mention of her dad's hated company again.

"Not everyone is opposed," Mrs. Stewart said mildly. "Some people think a resort would be good for jobs."

Patty snorted. "A few jobs in exchange for ruining our peaceful environment? It wouldn't be worth it. There are other ways of generating new jobs."

Like Joe's proposed B&B, Nina thought. He'd need to hire extra staff, and the kind of guests Joe wanted to attract would likely spend more money in the area, too.

"What do you think of the resort?" Mrs. Stewart asked Nina.

She looked up at the two women. "It shouldn't happen. It has to be stopped." Because Joe's dream had to come true.

Patty and Mrs. Stewart exchanged looks. "See?" Patty said. "Everyone thinks it's a terrible idea."

Fortunately, they dropped the subject after that.

. . .

"Should I lie low until we get to your place?" Nina's eyes sparked with mischief as she squirmed in the passenger seat of Joe's pickup truck. It was broad daylight, and he had just picked her up from the inn after she'd helped Mrs. Stewart. "I could put my head on your lap," she said, licking her lips. "That way no one would know I was with you."

Lust surged through Joe at the prospect of having those luscious lips of Nina's so close to his crotch. But he manfully tamped down his desires.

"Sweet pea, it's sweet of you to offer, but I don't want the sheriff pulling me over, because I'm sure I can't drive straight with your head in my lap."

Laughter bubbled out of her. "Well, as long as you don't mind being spotted with me."

He'd been careful to park at the back of the inn when he'd picked her up, and now instead of driving down the main street, he was taking a detour through the quiet part of town. He didn't particularly enjoy keeping his affair with Nina a secret, but he knew he had to be careful.

"If anyone asks," Joe said, "we're picking up supplies for the inn."

"Good thinking."

But she seemed a little deflated, as if the secrecy was getting to her. He lobbed her a quick glance, noticing the gold glimmers in her hair and the soft poutiness of her lower lip, and his blood stirred again. He could stare at her all day and never get his fill. She'd surprised him over the last few days, the way she'd leaped in so enthusiastically to help him without a second thought. His heart warmed once again.

Impulsively, he reached over and squeezed her free hand. "Thanks for all your help with the B&B."

She grinned sheepishly back at him. "You've said thank you already. You don't have to keep saying it. And besides, I wasn't the only one. You had your friends there, and they probably helped you more."

"Yeah, but I expect them to turn up, not you."

He thought of Deanne, the woman who had made him steer clear of any further relationships, and how different she was from Nina. Deanne would never have come out in a storm to help him. She wouldn't have supported his dream of opening a B&B at all.

Nina was gazing at him rather penetratingly. "You keep yourself so busy all the time," she said, blue eyes trained on him. "Is that how you avoid having a girlfriend?"

Startled by her question, Joe almost drove off the road. When he was back in control, he shook his head at her. "You know, you really shouldn't spring a question like that on a guy when he's driving."

"Sorry," she said, clearly unapologetic. "I'm just curious."

He clamped his hands around the steering wheel. "Clearly, you're not helping the cause."

She waved a hand. "I'm not auditioning for the part, but I'd like to know. A guy like you…stable, driven, knows what he wants and goes after it. You seem more like the type to be in a steady relationship, not bouncing around from affair to affair." She lifted her shoulders. "But you don't have to tell me. I know I'm too blunt sometimes."

He had no reason not to tell her about Deanne, now. He was over the hurt—nothing but scar tissue left.

"I broke up with my last girlfriend, Deanne, a few years back, just after my nonna's accident," he said calmly. "She'd cheated on me. When I confronted her, she said it was my fault because I spent too much time on my grandmother and my business."

Nina gasped. "What a bitch! But you shouldn't let her ruin your whole life."

"Who said she ruined my life? I'm very happy without a girlfriend."

"Don't you want to get married one day and have kids?"

He gave her a wry smile. "You really don't mind asking personal questions, do you?"

"Hey, you and I are way past the polite stage, if we were ever there at all."

"Agreed. The truth is I don't have time for a girlfriend, let alone a wife and kids. I'm busy enough as it is, and I'll be even more stretched when I get the loan for my B&B."

The justifications slipped from his tongue, glib and practiced. How often had he used these excuses? They sounded so plausible he almost believed them himself. But deep down he knew he would move heaven and earth not to allow anything to get between him and his woman. If she was the right woman, that was.

Nina rolled her shoulders, as if she wanted to shake off the somber mood that had come over them. "Well, seeing as you're such a busy beaver, we'd better make the most of this afternoon, huh?"

Joe was more than happy to push aside his serious thoughts. He squeezed her thigh and left his hand there. "Beaver, hmm? You read my mind."

She slapped his hand, feigning outrage. "Your mind is

so dirty."

"Yeah, but you like it."

She walked her fingers up his forearm, making his skin tingle. "Yeah, I do."

But when they reached his house, getting naked with her wasn't the first thing on his mind.

"I've got something for you," he said as they walked into his living room.

She reached for him and put her arms around his neck. "I know," she hummed, fitting his leg between her thighs and rubbing herself against him. "I've been looking forward to it."

"Now who's got the dirty mind?" He pressed his thigh up against her tight-fitting jeans and contemplated shuffling his priorities before reluctantly straightening his leg. "Behave yourself."

"You behave yourself." She pouted.

He stared at her lips, momentarily distracted, then shook his head and moved over to the couch where he picked up a large gift bag. He held it out to her.

"Hope you like it," he said, feeling oddly self-conscious.

She didn't grab the bag at once. "You bought me a gift?" She seemed stunned, as if she'd never received a present before. Accepting the gift bag, she continued to stare at him.

Joe shifted on his feet. "Open it."

Finally she peeked into the bag and pulled out a box, which she opened. A delighted smile lit up her face as she drew out a pair of sturdy black-and-gray sneakers.

"I don't believe it! This is just what I need!" She bounced on her toes like a kid on Christmas Day. "Oh, thank you, thank you, Joe!"

"I bought you some socks, too." Joe couldn't stop the smile cracking his face. He didn't think she'd be that pleased by his practical present.

"I can stop wearing my hideous Crocs!" She was wearing her cowboy boots now, but she heeled them off and put on the sneakers. She pranced around his living room, leaping from one foot to the other. "I've been meaning to buy a decent pair of shoes all week, but I never got the chance. When did you do this?"

"I drove into Fort Bragg this morning. I got your shoe size from your Crocs. Hope you don't mind my sneaking into your room."

"How could I mind?" She spun around one more time, then came to a halt in front of him and grabbed both his hands. "Thank you, Joe." Emotion choked her voice. "No one's ever given me such a thoughtful gift. Really. Thank you."

Her face was flushed and her eyes overbright, and he didn't quite get why she was so emotional over his gift, but he was glad she liked it.

"You're welcome." He drew her into his arms and pressed a kiss on her forehead. Nina never ceased to amaze him. Most women he knew would have expected a gift of flowers or chocolates or even jewelry. But not Nina. She was unique.

She snuggled into his embrace, her supple body sliding against his, and the shoes faded to the back of his mind as his trigger-happy libido surged to the fore.

"Now," he murmured in her ear, taking a quick nibble at her earlobe. "I do have another package for you. A particularly large package. But we'll have to unwrap it in the bedroom." He scooped her into his arms and headed toward his bedroom. "And once you've got it unwrapped, I might even let you play with it."

. . .

They had sex three times in two hours. Blissfully exhausted, Nina fell asleep tangled up in Joe's big arms. When she woke, the bed was empty and the sun was setting. She slipped on one of Joe's T-shirts, used the bathroom, and then went in search of Joe.

She found him in the kitchen making a salad. When he saw her, his hands grew still as his mouth fell open.

"That shirt looks sexy on you," he said, eyes hungrily eating her up as if the last few hours hadn't happened.

His T-shirt swamped her, reaching to her knees, but she did feel sexy in it, especially with his scent stamped into the fabric and onto her skin.

"Must be because I'm not wearing a bra." She sashayed over to him, then filched a cherry tomato from his salad bowl. "Whatcha doing?"

"Making dinner." Using his thumb, he swiped a drop of tomato juice from her lips. "Nothing fancy. Just steak and salad. Sound okay?"

"Sounds divine." She was famished. "Anything I can do to help?"

"How about fixing us some drinks? There's beer and wine in the fridge."

She opened a bottle of beer for him and poured herself a glass of white wine. Joe was neat and competent in his kitchen. He put sourdough rolls in the oven to heat up and grilled two thick New York steaks to juicy perfection. They ate in the dining alcove off the kitchen, where Joe had a wooden table and Shaker-style chairs.

Nina couldn't remember when a lover had cooked her a meal before. And she couldn't remember when she'd last felt so relaxed and comfortable. Some would say his house was modest, but to her it was honest and simple and everything you could wish for in a home.

They talked about Joe's plans for his B&B, about his grandmother and his sister. Finally, when their plates were empty, Joe leaned back in his chair and studied Nina with a speculative look.

"I feel like we've talked about me for way too long. What about you, Nina? Tell me something about yourself."

She was instantly on her guard. "Like what?"

"I don't know. Anything." He waved his beer bottle. "Any serious boyfriends in the past you want to blow off steam about?"

Oliver? She chewed her lip at the memories of her ex.

Joe rested his elbows on the table. "Hey," he said softly. "It was just a suggestion. You don't have to."

She met his eyes. "But if I didn't, that would mean I'm not over him, and I am. I am so over the bastard."

"A bastard, huh?"

"Yeah." She fiddled with her knife and fork as she wondered how much she could tell Joe without arousing his suspicion. "I don't want to go into the gory details. Suffice to say that I fell for Oliver. I thought he was special. I even thought he might be The One. But then I found out that he had ulterior motives for being with me. He didn't really care about me, just what I could do for him."

She pressed her lips together, surprised by the sudden

pang in her chest. Not because of Oliver, but because it hurt to know she wasn't as important as her money. That wound still festered in her soul.

Joe reached for her hands and squeezed them, his fingers warm and gentle. "He sounds like a complete jerk, but if there's one thing I know about you, Nina, it's that you're a fighter. Forget about him. He's pond scum. Don't let him sour the rest of your life."

The tenderness in his face broke her, and emotion stung the back of her throat. Joe was the complete antithesis of her ex. Just based on what he'd done for her this afternoon — buying her a thoughtful gift, pleasing her in bed, cooking her dinner, making her the focus of his attention — Joe cared more for her than her ex ever had.

Joe was wonderful. A man in a million. A man she could fall head over heels in love with —

Love?

Her heart seemed to stall for several beats. She started to cough and couldn't stop.

"Nina? Are you all right?" Joe got up to fetch her a glass of water.

As she spluttered, she gave herself a severe talking-to. No way could she let herself fall in love with Joe. Not when she was hiding such huge secrets from him. The guilt welled up again, more biting than before.

"Thanks," she whispered hoarsely after she'd drunk the water and recovered herself.

He patted her shoulder, still looking concerned. "Sorry," he said. "Didn't mean to get you all worked up over your ex."

"It doesn't matter."

"I've got ice cream." He smiled. "Chocolate chip and raspberry swirl."

"Why didn't you say so earlier?"

While Joe busied himself getting the ice cream, Nina hauled in several deep breaths to steady herself. She really couldn't fall in love with Joe. Not when she was concealing so much from him. In the brief time she had left, she would guard her heart. She would not let herself get hurt again.

Chapter Nine

"Got your wine orders figured out for the festival?" Joe asked Vince.

Joe was sitting in the bar with Vince and Sarah while they went over their preparations for the Hartley Food and Wine Festival. The days were ticking down fast, and he had so many other tasks to complete that he felt he'd been neglecting business at the Comet Inn.

While Vince went over the wine, Joe couldn't help sneaking a glance at the other side of the room, where Nina was busy wiping down tables and chairs. She was making slow progress, but he noticed she was thorough.

He pulled his attention back to the meeting to find Sarah eyeing him suspiciously.

"Sounds great," Joe said. He knew he could count on Vince to keep the bar side of things running smoothly. In fact, when he finally got his bank loan, he intended to ask Vince to be his manager at the inn so that he could concentrate on getting his B&B up and running.

Sarah began reading out the menu she had planned for the festival. They would be serving lunch and dinner over the three-day weekend and would need plenty of fresh supplies.

"Sorry to interrupt," Nina said as she walked toward them. "I couldn't help overhearing Sarah's menu."

Sarah pursed her lips. "And what? You don't approve?" Her voice dripped frost.

"No, it sounds delicious, but—" Nina darted a look at Vince then Joe. "I was thinking maybe you could plan a menu around craft beer."

"Plan a menu around craft beer?" Sarah sounded like Nina had suggested serving cow dung. "My food does not go *around* anything. My food is the reason why people come here to eat."

Nina toyed with the cloth in her hand. "Sorry, I didn't word that correctly. I meant a menu that would be complemented by craft beer. It's something different, don't you think? So many people love their craft beer, and we have some great microbreweries right in this area. It would be another way of highlighting local producers. What do you think, Joe?"

Sarah's expression was thunderous, but Joe knew that was partly because, for some reason, she disliked Nina. He rubbed his jaw as he mulled over Nina's suggestion.

"We've never done something like that before," he said to Sarah and Vince. "Might be worth trying, yeah?"

His head chef spluttered. "I've been working on my menu for days and now you want to change it just because of *her*?"

Joe's shoulders stiffened. Sarah was superbly talented,

but her ego and mistrust sometimes got the better of her. Plus, he didn't care for the way she treated Nina so dismissively. He was about to say something stern to her when Nina broke in.

"I don't think you'd have to change your menu that much," she said. "You're already planning curries and pheasant and pulled pork. They just need to be paired with the best beer, right, Vince?"

"Yeah, that shouldn't be too hard." Vince appeared enthusiastic.

"Vince knows all about microbrewing." Nina grinned at him. "In fact, he has his own craft beer you could feature at the festival."

Both Joe and Sarah looked at Vince. The bartender's ears turned red. "Nina, I don't think I—"

"Of course you do." She turned to Joe. "Vince has upgraded his backyard operation to commercial grade. You should taste his beer. It's really good."

"Commercial grade? Why didn't you tell me?" Joe asked Vince.

Vince shrugged. "You're busy enough as it is. And I don't like tooting my own horn. But if you'd like to try some…?"

Joe nodded, and Vince jumped to his feet. He hurried behind the bar counter and returned with a bottle and a couple of glasses. After carefully decanting the beer, he passed glasses to Joe and Sarah.

The beer had a distinctive chewy, hoppy flavor. It wasn't Joe's preference, but he knew it would appeal to aficionados. "That's really great, Vince."

Sarah pursed her lips. "Yeah, I could see it going with a spicy dish," she said almost reluctantly.

"It's decided, then." Joe nodded at Vince and Sarah. "Can you two thrash out the details and come up with a menu and supply list?"

"Just me and Vince? Sure you don't want Nina to help us?" Sarah snarked.

Joe gave her a sharp stare, conveying his disapproval, until Sarah turned brick red. "If you can't get it done by the end of today, then maybe you will need Nina's help."

"We'll get it done," Sarah muttered, looking crestfallen.

"Good." Joe pushed to his feet and gathered up his notes. "I'll leave you guys to it, then."

He headed out the bar only to find Nina had followed behind. When he stopped and turned, she seemed apologetic.

"I'm sorry for causing friction," she said. "I didn't realize Sarah would resent me that much."

Joe shook his head. "Don't be sorry. I appreciate your input." He tilted his head to study her more closely. "How long has this idea been brewing inside that head of yours?"

"Oh, a few days. You really think it's a good idea?"

"It's a great idea, and I'm glad you forced Vince to fess up about his craft beer. He's too modest sometimes."

Joe felt guilty that his busyness had prevented Vince from approaching him about his beers, so he was extra glad that Nina had pushed Vince. Nina was good to her friends, and she displayed a surprisingly entrepreneurial spirit.

"I'm really looking forward to this festival now," Nina said.

"I wish I had an extra week before it happens. There's so much stuff I still need to do."

She glanced around the empty reception lobby before stepping closer and tracing a circle over his shirt, causing his heart to thump in anticipation.

"Will you be too busy to visit me tonight?" She slanted him a flirty look from beneath her eyelashes.

He swallowed as lust, so easily triggered when she was around, flooded his veins. "Not too busy."

He might have a million things to do, but nothing could stanch his thirst for her.

•••

Joe yawned as his beeping cell phone alarm woke him. A steely gray predawn dimness filled Nina's room. Beside him, Nina stirred as he tried to extricate himself from the sheets. Her single bed hadn't bothered him when he'd reached her room last night, and the tangled, sweaty sex they'd enjoyed had been as intense as ever. But the few hours' sleep he'd caught afterward had been fractured and cramped.

Now, his lower back twinged as he carefully levered himself off the bed, trying not to wake Nina. But she was already blinking at him.

"Go back to sleep," he whispered, stroking her hair away from her forehead. "It's still early. I need to get home."

She yawned and stretched like a cat, the sheet twisted around her naked body. Ignoring his stirring cock, Joe reached for his clothes.

"What are you up to today?" Extending her arms above her head, Nina arched her back. Her creamy breasts tempted him.

"I need to buy more hardware for the B&B." He tried not to stare at her pink nipples as he pulled on his jeans and T-shirt. "And after lunch I'm visiting my nonna."

"Do you always visit her on a Wednesday?"

"Every Wednesday and Sunday, bar an emergency." He sat on the bed to lace up his shoes.

Nina sat up, too, curled behind him as she watched him do his shoelaces. "Can I come with you?" she asked.

He turned to her in surprise. "Why?"

She shrugged diffidently. "She obviously means a lot to you. And I kinda miss my own grandmother."

He was even more surprised. "You do?"

"Yes. She's the only one in my family who understands me." She drew her knees up to her chest, changing from siren to child. "But you don't have to take me if you don't want."

"You can come," he said on impulse. He ruffled her hair, slightly confused by the sudden change in her. "I'll see you later, then."

• • •

From her armchair by the window, Nonna Lina looked at Nina with shy curiosity before she glanced at Joe sitting next to Nina.

"She's a nice girl, your friend," she said to Joe. "But much too thin. She doesn't eat enough."

Neither do you, Nina thought with concern. Joe's grand-mother was painfully thin, though she seemed in good spirits. Joe had told her his nonna had always been a ball of energy, an active, typical Italian grandmother who'd doted on Joe and his sister, but the car accident had left her perma-nently altered. She didn't recognize many of her old friends and was afraid of sudden changes, so Joe's regular visits were vital to her.

"Don't worry, Nonna," Joe said. "She eats plenty."

"Oh?" Nonna Lina cocked her head. "Bring her to dinner next time. I'll make her my rigatoni beef ragù. Your favorite dish."

"I'm sure she'll love it." Joe smiled, but when he met Nina's gaze his eyes were sad. Nonna Lina didn't realize it, but her days of making rigatoni beef ragù were long gone.

"Why doesn't Deanne visit?" Nonna Lina suddenly asked Joe.

"I broke up with Deanne a while ago, Nonna," he said quietly. It was plain that his grandmother had asked him this question many times before.

"Broke up?" Nonna Lina's hands trembled. "But who'll look after you?"

"I can look after myself. I'm fine, Nonna."

It took Joe a while to reassure her.

A few minutes later, their visit was over. Joe was silent as they walked out of the nursing home.

"She seems well cared for there," Nina said, wishing there was more she could say to comfort him.

Joe gave her an absentminded smile as they got into his truck. "She's been at Pine Groves four years now. I can't move her." He started the engine and looked at Nina, his expression dark. "If I can't get my investment loan soon, I'll have to sell to Beaumont. I can't afford not to."

Guilt knotted her stomach at the mention of her dad. How she hated lying to Joe. Maybe there was a way of telling him the truth without losing his respect, but as yet she hadn't found it.

And somehow she had to help him get that loan and achieve his dream. How, she didn't know, either. Nina reached for his hand. "You'll get your loan. I'm sure of it."

He didn't speak, but he held her hand until they reached Hartley.

• • •

"Joe? What do you think?"

Prying open his blurry eyes, Joe blinked at Patty Williams, one of the committee members, who was tapping him on the forearm. "Hmm?"

"Did you fall asleep?" The older woman frowned.

Joe pushed himself upright in his chair and became aware of the others around the table staring at him in surprise. Damn, had he just nodded off during a meeting with the festival committee? He rubbed a hand over his face, suppressing a yawn. "Sorry. You were saying?"

Patty cocked her head to one side. "Are you all right, Joe? I've never seen you drop off like that. Had a late night, did you?"

He sure had. Last night he'd taken Nina home with him. His bed was definitely more comfortable to sleep in than hers, but they hadn't done much sleeping. They'd stayed up late again, then caught a few hours of exhausted sleep before he'd driven her back to the Comet Inn before dawn broke. He'd returned home, collapsed in bed again for an hour, and somehow managed to drag himself to the festival committee meeting, only to succumb to fatigue once he'd sat down.

"I'm fine," he said even as the muscles in his lower back twinged. Three late nights in a row. Three nights of incredible, hot sex. Now he was paying for it.

"Okay." Patty didn't look convinced. She pushed a

printout toward him, her expression still concerned. "Think you'll have time to review the financial statements? We really need your input."

Some of last night's euphoria ebbed away as guilt took over. He had a responsibility to the town, and he shouldn't allow this affair to distract him from his duties. The Food and Wine Festival was a huge deal for Hartley, and it deserved his proper attention. Instead, he was falling asleep on the job daydreaming about Nina.

He took the printed spreadsheet from Patty and assured everyone that he would go over the numbers before the end of the day. Soon after, the meeting broke up, and Joe headed to the Comet Inn, determined to be his professional best.

But his resolve was tested as soon as he encountered Nina in the hotel lobby chatting with Vince. When she spotted him, she flashed him a dimpled smile that tied his stomach and sent lust shooting through his veins.

"Hi," she murmured, a dreamy, sleepy look to her eyes as she twisted the mop handle.

"Hi," he replied, sounding husky.

Belatedly he realized Vince was studying them. Was it obvious that he and Nina couldn't stay away from each other? If Vince suspected, then it wouldn't take long for the others to notice it too, and he didn't want to have to deal with the possible fallout right now.

He schooled his face into a bland mask. "Hey, Vince. Everything okay here?"

"Sure," Vince replied. "Everything's fine *here*."

Damn, Vince did suspect something.

Nina gathered up her mop and bucket. "Better get going with my chores," she said, hurrying up the stairs.

It took an almighty effort for Joe not to stare after her. Vince was still eyeing him. Joe cleared his throat. "I'm going to Fort Bragg this afternoon. Got a meeting with another bank."

"Good. Maybe that'll keep your mind occupied." Vince walked off, leaving Joe to frown after him.

• • •

"And this is my spatchcock with sage and wild mushroom," Sarah announced as she laid a platter on the table where Nina was sitting with Vince and the other kitchen staff.

Vince sat up. "Let's see how it goes with the old ale, then."

Nina and the others had just finished the staff dinner, but Vince had saved his appetite to sample Sarah's dishes for the festival. Sarah placed some clean plates on the table.

"It looks delicious," Nina said, "but I'll let you experts try it first."

"Suit yourself." Sarah shrugged. She swiveled round and waved at Joe, who'd just entered the restaurant. "Come and try my spatchcock."

As Joe walked toward them, Nina couldn't keep her eyes off him. After three late nights spent with him she'd been lethargic all day, but suddenly she was wide-awake.

Joe wore a business suit because of his bank meeting in Fort Bragg. His jacket was slung over his arm, revealing a soft gray dress shirt and close-fitting charcoal pants. Joe in corporate attire was just as smoking hot as Joe in jeans and a T-shirt. Nina's brain turned woozy as she imagined running her hands over his shirt and pants, feeling his muscles bunch up beneath the fabric. She curled her fingers into her palms as she struggled to contain her fantasies.

"How did your meeting at the bank go?" Vince asked Joe.

"Don't ask." A vexed look passed over Joe's face but was quickly gone. "I need food. Looks like I arrived at the right time."

Sarah motioned for Joe to sit next to her, but instead he rounded the table and slid into the chair beside Nina. His nearness set her body humming, the attraction sparking and pulling her into his thrall. She drew in a breath to steady herself, but instead inhaled a whiff of Joe's crisp cologne that went straight to her head.

Sarah frowned but continued to divide the spatchcock into three portions. She passed plates to Vince and Joe. When Joe saw Nina had been left out, he turned to her, his eyebrows lifted in query.

"I'll let you three be the judge," she said, striving to sound normal.

Joe sampled the spatchcock and nodded at Sarah. "This is incredible." He ate another mouthful and sipped at the old ale beer. "Amazing how the beer complements all the flavors." He nodded at Sarah and Vince. "Great work, guys. Sarah, I think this is going to be one of your signature dishes."

Sarah went pink. "Thanks. I've been working really hard to get it right."

Joe turned to Nina. "You should taste this, seeing as it was all your idea." He forked up a morsel of meat and held it to her. "Here, have some of mine."

Nina blinked at him in surprise. Beneath the table, his knee nudged against hers, causing her thigh to quiver. The glint in his eyes told her it was no accident. So, Joe wanted to tease her in front of his staff? Well, two could play that game.

Angling forward, she wrapped her fingers around his hand and guided his fork into her mouth. She let the fork slowly glide out past her lips, all the while keeping her gaze locked on Joe, her provocation deliberate. A spark flared in his eyes. He pressed the length of his thigh against hers, and she almost choked on her mouthful of food. Oh, Joe was too good at this game. As she leaned back in her chair, flushed and aroused, she realized everyone at the table was staring at them.

Sarah pulled a face. "Are you two finished?"

Vince coughed uncomfortably. "I'd better get back to the bar." He pushed to his feet and hurried out of the restaurant. The other staff members scattered, too, except for Sarah.

Nina swallowed her mouthful of spatchcock. "It's, er, delicious."

"Really?" Sarah was giving her the stink eye again. "How could you tell when you gulped it down in one second?"

Joe cleared his throat. "Sarah…" he warned in a low voice.

Thoroughly discomfited by the situation, Nina pushed to her feet and grabbed the empty plates. "I'd better get these to the kitchen," she said, and beat a hasty retreat.

As the evening wore on and the place got busier, Nina concentrated on her work and pushed all thoughts of Joe to the back of her mind. She hoped the incident with the spatchcock would be forgotten but knew it was a vain hope when, later that night as she stepped out the backyard with two bags of garbage, Sarah's tall figure loomed up beside her like a prison guard.

Still, Nina tried to keep the atmosphere neutral. "Lovely

night tonight." She walked toward the Dumpster, tilting her head up to the sky. "Look at all those stars."

Sarah kept pace with her, ignoring the stars. "What's going on with you and Joe?" she asked bluntly.

"Nothing's going on," Nina insisted. Technically, that was true. Joe hadn't made any promises. And she didn't want any. She opened the Dumpster and heaved the first bag in.

"Bullshit. Are you and Joe having an affair?"

Nina stood her ground. "That's none of your business."

"It is my business. Joe's my friend. I won't stand by and let an oversexed tramp mess him around."

Nina gasped. "Oversexed tramp! You've got one helluva nerve calling me names."

Sarah stepped closer, tall and menacing. "You talked Joe into hiring you when you're obviously unqualified. You've been here two weeks and already he's drooling over you. You've schemed and seduced your way in here, and you're up to no good. Of course you're an oversexed tramp."

Nina let out a furious laugh. "Ha! If I'm such an oversexed tramp, then why am I the one taking out the garbage?"

"It's all a stunt, a cover. You're not really here because of the job. Anyone can see that. There's something else going on."

Indignation boiled in Nina. "I might not be as quick as everyone else, but I pull my weight around here, and even you can't deny that. As for Joe, he's a big boy. He can take care of himself. He doesn't need a mother hen like you flapping around him."

Sarah gasped and faltered back as if Nina had pushed her. For a few seconds she appeared to struggle for breath.

"Joe takes care of everyone else, but he needs someone

watching out for him." Sarah sniffed and fisted her hands. "And I am not his mother hen."

Nina bit her lower lip as the truth sunk in. *Oh, shit.* Sarah had a crush on Joe, and he probably had no clue. No wonder Sarah was so ready to bite her head off. Nina and Joe had shamelessly flirted over the spatchcock right in front of Sarah, and that must have hurt. If she found out that Nina had been spending nights with Joe... Nina's animosity against Sarah subsided.

"Look, I appreciate your concern for Joe, but he's in no danger from me."

Sarah shook her head morosely. "You don't convince me. I knew you were trouble the moment I saw you."

Nina sighed, her patience slipping. "Well, maybe you should speak to Joe instead of me." She tossed the second garbage bag into the Dumpster and slammed the lid shut. "I'm going back inside."

The other woman glowered at her. "I know you're hiding something, Nina, and sooner or later I'll find out what it is."

Nina shrugged and left the yard. If Sarah only knew how her secret was weighing on her... How much longer could she continue deceiving Joe?

Joe had been nothing but open and honest with her. He didn't deserve to be lied to. But if she told him the truth, Joe would surely despise her, and that prospect was too much to bear.

• • •

Nina retreated to her bedroom as soon as her hectic evening shift was over. After her confrontation with Sarah, she didn't think it would be appropriate to hang around in the bar waiting for Joe, especially since she found it impossible to hide her attraction to him. She should try to curb her libido. It was crazy sleeping with a man who didn't know her true identity. Crazier still to have these strange, warm feelings whenever she thought about him. All things considered, it was better to be alone tonight.

But all her sensible ideas scattered when, an hour later, she heard someone walk up to her room. The footsteps paused outside her door, and she knew instinctively that it was Joe standing on the other side. Her breathing hitched as she waited for him to knock. *Please, please, please knock.* Her desperation for Joe shocked her. Before she could help herself, she moved to the door and opened it.

Joe blinked at her, making her conscious of her scrubbed face and the fact she wore only a T-shirt. His dark eyes warmed, and the glow in them chased away her reservations. Yes, she felt increasingly guilty over her deception, but she wasn't lying about how she felt about him.

And what exactly are those feelings? a critical voice queried at the back of her mind. *This is supposed to be just some harmless fun, isn't it?*

The nagging voice faded as she took in Joe's presence, delighted at his visit.

"Are you just going to stand there," she said, "or are you coming in?"

His gaze swept over her T-shirt, making her nipples perk up in anticipation. "I shouldn't be here," he said.

She smiled. "No, you shouldn't be." But he was. She took him by the hand and tugged him toward the bed.

"Tired?" she asked and sat next to him.

"A little. It's been a busy day."

She recalled his bank meeting earlier that hadn't gone well, and bit her lip. To help ease her conscience, she shifted behind him and squeezed his shoulders. "Want a massage?"

"That'd be great." He sounded surprised.

She began working on his muscles, kneading the tight knots in his back and shoulders. Joe groaned in relief, lowering his head. The sight of his bowed head made her heart twinge in a novel way. She was only giving him a massage, and yet it felt more than that. It felt as if he was letting down his barriers, allowing her into his citadel. She slid her palms over him, relishing the flex of his muscles, the scent of his skin. She wanted to do this every night. Wanted to be the one he turned to for comfort at the end of a tiring day.

Her heart panged with deep longing.

But how could she ever have that without telling him the truth? Maybe—her mind quavered—it was time to fess up. Not now when he was at ease and relaxed, but maybe later…sometime soon.

Joe sighed. "I should go home."

No, she almost cried out. She wanted every drop of him while she could, because who knew how long this would last? "Why?"

"I have spreadsheets to go over."

Her body took over, reckless with yearning. Rising to her feet, she spread her legs over his knees. "I have a spreadsheet for you to go over, too. Figures that need massaging…"

He ran a hand along the length of her thigh, the glint in his eye mirroring the fire in her veins. "I'm good at massaging figures." She quivered as he slid his hand higher under her T-shirt and pulled her down to sit astride his knees.

"W-wonderful." She clutched at his shoulders. "What about bottom lines? Any good at those?"

Laughing, he leaned in to nibble her earlobe. "Sweet pea, I'm all over your bottom line. It's one of your prime assets." Shifting his hand up, he cupped her bare breast, causing them both to breathe faster. "Along with these…"

She hissed with pleasure. "That's some dirty bookkeeping you have in mind."

He lifted her and pushed her onto the bed, pressing the full weight of his body onto her as he covered her mouth with his.

"Just wait until we get to double-entry accounting, sweet pea."

Chapter Ten

"You haven't looked at the spreadsheets?" Patty Williams blinked in complete bafflement. "But Joe, the festival's next week, and you *promised*."

Guilt and embarrassment crawled over Joe as he faced his colleague. Those budgets and costing were vital for the festival. He'd let Patty and the committee down, all because he couldn't keep his priorities straight recently.

"Sorry, Patty. I'll go over them as soon as I can."

The older woman glanced around the lobby of the Comet Inn, where several people stood about, some waiting to check in, others browsing the tourist brochure stand. The inn was booked with guests invited to a weekend wedding, and the restaurant would be hosting a prewedding dinner that night.

"Doesn't look like you'll get a chance today," Patty said through a sigh.

Joe grimaced. He hated reneging on his word. This was

all his fault. He shouldn't have gone to Nina's room last night.

"I'll get on it today, I guarantee."

Patty nodded, though doubt lingered in her expression. She took her leave, and he went back to seeing to his paying guests.

Later, Joe retreated to his office to study the spreadsheets. He couldn't let Patty down a second time. After a couple of hours of intense concentration, he'd finished his analysis, made several corrections and emailed the revised spreadsheets to the committee. Relieved, he told himself there'd be no more slipups from his end. This festival was too important to mess up. Tourists brought in revenue, and he needed every extra cent for his B&B.

· · ·

The sound of breaking glass made Joe wince as his trainee bartender dropped a full bottle of single malt whisky. At a nearby table, a disgruntled customer pulled a face at the scorched patty in his hamburger. Joe approached the man— one of his regulars—and whisked the burger away, telling him his meal would be on the house. He gave instructions to one of the kitchen staff to get the man a replacement burger, then returned to the bar, where Vince was overseeing the trainee and his mess.

"What's going on tonight?" Joe asked Vince when they had a moment alone. "Everyone's dropping things, mixing up orders, burning food. Is there a full moon or something?"

Vince picked up a cloth and began wiping the bar counter. "You can't guess?" he said, almost sullen. "He'd been unusually clammed up all evening.

"No." Joe looked him in the eye. "You going to tell me?"

His friend paused his polishing. "You really can't guess why everyone's acting weird? It's because of you and Nina."

Joe's stomach muscles tensed. "What about me and Nina?"

"You know." Vince shrugged. "All that flirting going on between you two."

Joe's mind raced.

"You mean yesterday with the spatchcock? That was nothing."

"It wasn't nothing. You were practically making out in front of everyone. And it's not just the spatchcock. Every time you and Nina are in the same place together it's like happy hour at a pickup joint. You've got a thing for her, and don't even try to deny it."

The truculent tone in his friend's voice irked Joe, but he kept his own voice steady as he said, "Are you jealous? Thinking you want a crack at her, too?"

Vince's cheeks grew ruddy. "I like Nina, but we're just friends. That's not why I'm pissed off." He rubbed at a spot on the counter vigorously. "You must have noticed how upset Sarah was when you started fooling around with Nina at the table. Sarah's bad mood affects everyone around here. Hence the accidents happening tonight. Sarah's never liked Nina, and you made things worse by agreeing to Nina's idea about the craft beer thing."

"But it's a good idea." Joe stared at Vince. "And she did it for you, you ass."

"I'm grateful for that, but to Sarah it looked like you only agreed because you want to fool around with Nina."

"I don't see how it's any of Sarah's business who I fool around with."

"Come off it, Joe. You know better than that."

Vince moved down the counter to serve a customer, leaving Joe to brood over what he'd just said. Joe rubbed his hand over his face, feeling like a jerk. Yeah, he'd been aware for some time that Sarah had a soft spot for him, but he didn't think it was serious; she kept it well hidden, and he'd never thought others would notice. But apparently Vince had.

He waited until Vince was free before drawing him aside where they couldn't be overheard.

"Look," Joe said quietly. "Whatever you suspect about Sarah, keep it to yourself. She and I have never talked about it, and I get the impression she'd like to keep it that way."

Vince cocked his head to one side. "She'd be a good match for you, you know."

Joe compressed his lips. "You also know I'm not interested in a relationship."

"So this thing going on with Nina—it's just a casual hookup?"

"It's not a hookup. It's…" An obsession. A compulsion that grabbed him and overwhelmed all his usual rationality. He thrust his fingers through his hair in frustration.

God damn it. Why did everything have to be so complicated? He wanted Nina so badly at times he couldn't think about anything except the need to touch her, pleasure her, take her. Didn't matter how many times he had her, it was never enough.

Nina was like a carnival that had sprung up out of nowhere on the side of the road, luring him with her bright lights and crazy rides and cotton candy. Distracting him from the journey he'd mapped out for himself. But it wasn't her fault he kept putting his desire for her ahead of everything else. That was all on him. He just wished there was a way he could stay at the carnival without straying off course.

"So you do admit you're involved with Nina," Vince persisted.

Joe shrugged. It felt like he was being backed into a corner. "I'm not big on semantics. Whatever it is, it's temporary. You know me, Vince. Since when do I have the time for anything serious?" He was on firmer ground here. Everyone knew he was too busy for a girlfriend. His track record spoke for itself.

"You sure you're not playing with fire here?"

"Don't worry about me, man. I can handle it."

Vince threw him a skeptical look. "If you say so."

Of course he could handle a fling. He was a man with experience in brief relationships, and whatever label he put on this thing with Nina, he knew it could only be temporary, because carnivals always moved on. They brought fun and excitement for a short while and then disappeared as quickly as they arrived. They never put down permanent roots. So he and Nina would enjoy a few wild nights—or maybe more—before she packed up and moved back to the city. That was the most likely scenario. And sure, he admitted his obsession with her was causing a few problems with his friends here at the inn, and that was affecting his staff, too, but he had the situation under control. For a few more nights, the hassle was worth it. Right?

• • •

Mindful of the minor rebellion among his staff, Joe avoided Nina the rest of that Friday and went home by himself, where he spent a restless night alone, horny and frustrated. The next day was no better. As soon as he laid eyes on Nina sweeping the barroom floor, he wanted to bend her over one of the tables and have his way with her.

He managed to stay away from her for several hours, but later, as he emerged from his office, he spotted Nina entering one of the storage rooms at the end of the hall. He hesitated, aware of how full the inn was, but the thought of being alone with Nina was too damn irresistible. He scanned the area for witnesses then quickly followed her into the room.

Nina whirled around as the door clicked shut. "Oh. Hi. I'm here for napkins." She seemed surprised to see him.

He drew in a breath, and her scent pulled him in. Avoiding her last night had done him no good at all. He still wanted her, more desperately than before. So desperately that he was willing to risk discovery.

"I missed you last night." The huskiness in his voice echoed his need.

She widened her eyes. "I missed you, too."

Their eyes met, and the fuse between them crackled alight, drawing him in, licking fire in his veins.

The overhead glow picked out the golden tips of her hair and the soft curve of her lower lip. He'd meant to pull her into his arms, but something about her made him pause. She was like porcelain china, delicate yet strong, exquisite and durable at the same time. He traced the contours of her face with his fingers, marveling at her bone structure.

"Did I ever tell you you're incredibly beautiful?" he said.

She drew in a breath. "You've called me a lot of things."

Beneath his fingers, a pulse in her temple fluttered. "But never incredibly beautiful."

"Well, you are." He hesitated, confused at how a simple urge to kiss her had morphed into something more complex. "But you probably hear that all the time."

"Not as often as you imagine." Stepping up to him, she slid her hands up his chest, bringing them to rest at his shoulders. "If you think I'm beautiful, it's because of you." A shy smile lifted her lips. "When you touch me, I feel amazing."

"Yeah?" He snaked an arm around her waist to haul her in. "Guess I'd better touch you some more, huh?"

He bent his head and took her mouth with his. The kiss was fiery, explosive, far hotter than he'd expected. Kissing Nina awakened something deeper in him, something that went beyond animal lust. As he moved from her lips to explore her smooth, delectable neck, Nina purred a thrilling moan that jolted him into fierce action like a shot of nitro.

He pushed her up against the wall, lifting her at the waist so she could wrap her legs around him. He kissed her neck, at the same time working one hand under her T-shirt. Her torso quivered and tensed as his fingers glided over her soft skin. When he reached her bra, her legs tightened around his hips as she arched her back. He pushed up her bra, and as his hand closed over her breast, he grew light-headed from lack of oxygen.

Despite the fuzziness, something niggled at the back of his mind, making him lift his lips from her honeyed mouth. "This doesn't seem right," he muttered, not sure what he was thinking.

She rubbed her pelvis up and down against him. "Feels very right to me…" Her syrupy voice dripped with arousal.

He gave a brief laugh. "No, I mean doing it here in the storeroom."

"Oh? You want to lock the door?"

The idea of taking Nina against the shelves excited him, but was that good enough for her? She was luscious and beautiful and about the most amazing woman he'd ever met. Surely she deserved more than what he was offering?

He became aware of his hand absently fondling her breast, and her nipple warm and erect in his palm. Damn, he wanted her so badly, but maybe he wanted more from her than just sex. The thought made him pause.

"Joe?" Uncertainty flickered in her eyes.

He pushed his confusion away and concentrated on Nina, on her ripe mouth, on the heat surging in both of them. "Shit, I don't have a condom," he said.

She sighed, clearly disappointed as she unwound her legs from his hips and stood. "I guess we need to be sensible." Then her eyes widened as he began to undo the buttons of her jeans. "What are you doing?"

"Being sensible." He grinned, watching her intently as he slid his hand inside her jeans. For a moment her expression was blank with surprise, then, as he caressed her lower belly, her eyelids drooped to half-mast.

"Mmm...I like your sensibility. Oh—" She gasped as he cupped her mound.

He drank in the woozy look on her face. This felt better, giving instead of taking. With his free hand, he reclaimed her breast and teased her nipple, simultaneously sliding his finger into her swollen folds, stroking her until her cheeks were flushed and her eyes were groggy with intoxication. God, she was so mesmerizing. He wanted to lavish her with pleasure, to make her the center of his world, to give her everything he had. With his gaze fixed on her, he slid two fingers deep into her, increasing his rhythm, discovering what turned her on. She heaved and melted until her body tensed up, and she moaned aloud as orgasmic color bloomed across her neck and face. When her shudders subsided, he slowly withdrew his hands from her and straightened her clothes.

"Oh, Joe…" Her face wore a blissed-out glow as she ruffled her hair. "That was"—she drew in a shaky breath—"stupendous." Smiling, she ran her fingers down his chest, bringing them to rest at the belt holding up his jeans. "I can be sensible with you, too."

His blood leaped at the thought of Nina going down on him, but not now. Pleasuring her was its own reward. Besides, they'd been in here too long, and someone might come in.

Holding her hands, he lifted them to his mouth. "Thanks, but I'll take a rain check on that."

"Oh? You don't want—"

"I want it. God, do I want it." He took a deep breath as his lust threatened to overcome his common sense. "But later tonight." He swallowed. "Back at my place. Right now, we both should get back to work."

"Okay." She curled her arms around him, raised herself on tiptoe, and crushed her mouth against his. Her tongue darted into his mouth, bold with promise, before she released him and stepped back. "I'll see you later."

Tonight couldn't come soon enough.

Chapter Eleven

Joe trudged into the changing sheds, the last of his soccer team to stagger off the field, and collapsed onto a bench, feeling like he'd been run over by a garbage truck.

Mick, his sweaty teammate drooping opposite him, shot him a gloomy look. "We were hammered out there today."

Joe couldn't deny that. "Yeah. They outplayed us." Wearily he began unlacing his cleats.

"What happened to all those set moves we practiced? Why weren't you feeding me any good balls?"

Joe shook his head. "I'm sorry. My mind was somewhere else."

"You can say that again. You couldn't even make it to the game on time."

It was the first time Joe had ever done that. He'd shown up five minutes after the start whistle — an unthinkable occurrence that had never happened before — and he'd played the entire game like a sleepwalker. He hadn't initiated any set moves, hadn't motivated his team when they began crumbling, hadn't done his job as the linchpin and captain of his team.

"Guess those talent scouts didn't see me at my best," Mick said with a dismal sigh.

Joe's head jerked up. "Shit. I forgot about them." Mick was the best striker Joe had ever played with. He was also desperate to escape his life at the family lumber mill, and he'd hoped the scouts visiting today would pick him out and offer him some hope.

Soccer was his lifeline, and Joe had screwed up his chances. "I'm sorry, Mick. I really fucked up."

Mick's dejected stance multiplied Joe's guilt. He'd screwed up the most important game of the year, and for what? He had no good excuse. The realization weighed heavily on him.

Mick grunted. "Hey, maybe next time, right?"

Next time. Next time, would he still be in the grip of his mad passion for Nina, or would it have died down just as quickly as it had flared up? He doubted his obsession with her would peter out any time soon. Not by last night's standards. Or this morning. When he'd dragged himself out of bed after another all-nighter, she'd begun to tease him and flirt with him, and he'd welcomed it, until all thought of soccer receded before the burning need to make good on her promises and bury himself in her.

His decision to stay with her had made him late for his match. He'd shattered his concentration and his game plans. This affair with Nina was beginning to seriously impact other areas of his life. It wasn't supposed to be like this. It was only supposed to be a secret, sizzling side order of sex. He wasn't supposed to let her take root in his mind so deeply as to change his routine.

He went home to tackle the avalanche of emails about the festival, but when he sat on his couch, he instantly fell asleep. Some time later, he woke up to find he'd slept several hours. And now he was late for visiting his nonna. Seriously late.

By the time he rushed into the nursing home, Nonna Lina was huddled in her armchair, twisting her blanket with shaking hands, while two caregivers tried to calm her. When she caught sight of Joe, she cried out.

"I thought you'd had a car accident!" She sobbed and collapsed against the cushions.

"I'm so sorry, Nonna." Joe hunkered down at her side. "I fell asleep."

Joe's heart was a guilty stone in his throat as he tried to reassure her that nothing was wrong. She wasn't convinced. He never missed a Sunday without giving her plenty of notice. How could he be late today without there being something very wrong?

It took Joe more than an hour to soothe her, and all the while he was conscious of the curious—and maybe accusing—glances from the caregivers.

As he held his nonna's bone-thin hand, her vulnerability hit him anew. He'd made a deathbed promise to his father to look after his grandmother, and that didn't mean just footing the bills. His uncle and aunt visited Nonna whenever they could, but they had their hands full with the farm and couldn't always get to town. And his sister loved visiting Nonna but was thousands of miles away. With her fragile grip on reality, Nonna relied on Joe and his regular visits to maintain her peace of mind. For the first time ever, he'd let her down, and she was devastated.

He couldn't let that happen again. He couldn't let an affair turn his life upside down. And the only way to accomplish that now was to shut it down completely.

• • •

Nina was taking a nap in her room when a knock on her door woke her. Rubbing her eyes, she opened her door to find Joe standing there. She smiled as her body immediately grew warm.

She leaned against the door. "Hi. Joining me for a nap?" After all the sex they'd enjoyed recently, she assumed they were both too worn-out for more, but it would be nice to cuddle together in her narrow bed.

But Joe shook his head curtly. "I need to discuss something with you."

Her heart sank at his gruff tone and the bleak set of his face. Joe hadn't come here to cuddle with her. He'd come here to break up with her. She knew it. Could hear it in his tone, could sense it in his uneasy stiffness, his braced expression. All the warmth fled from her body as she straightened, replaced by icy foreboding.

"Yeah, sure." She motioned for him to come inside, then moved away to perch on the edge of the desk.

Grim faced, Joe raked his fingers through his hair, looking like he was searching for the right words. Well, he'd have to do it on his own; she wasn't going to help him dump her… *Dump me. Oh, hell.* Suddenly her legs were shaky and the back of her mouth tasted bile.

"I was late visiting Nonna this afternoon."

Nina blinked. "I'm sorry."

His fisted knuckles whitened. "Nonna...well, she's never recovered from her car accident, physically or mentally. We've found it's best to have her follow a regular schedule. It keeps her calm and happy, but any deviation from that schedule without warning makes her anxious. And I mean extremely anxious. I was late today because I fell asleep at home."

"Because of last night." She rubbed her upper arms. "I didn't realize..."

Joe shook his head. "You're not to blame. I'm the one who's been dropping the ball lately."

She looked up at him. "So it's not just your grandmother?"

Sighing, he scowled down at his shoes. "I fell asleep at a festival meeting. I was late with some financial paperwork. And I missed the kickoff of my soccer match and played the crappiest game on record. I've let down people I care about, people who expect more from me."

The disapproval in his face pinched her. Joe had high standards, and he was disappointed in himself.

"Yeah," she said, "and let's not forget the Comet Inn. Sarah already hates my guts, and she doesn't even know we've been sleeping together."

Joe's face grew even grimmer. "Tell me about it. Vince isn't happy with me, either. In fact, everyone's been walking on eggshells around here."

Nina bit her lip as she realized how much damage this was causing Joe. Damn. He'd put his business at risk to be with her, the business he'd built from scratch and worked so hard at. The business that employed people and generated income for the town. The business that paid for his sister's college education and his grandmother's care.

Joe wasn't like Nina. He didn't have an inheritance or rich connections to fall back on. Everything he had he'd earned on his own. People relied on him. People needed him.

She turned to Joe, her throat tight. "Looks like we've been selfish, huh?"

He stared at her, then crossed the small room and held her shoulders. "We just got carried away." He paused and drew in a breath. "God, did we get carried away."

"But we should stop, shouldn't we?"

"Yeah, we should," Joe said, "even though I don't want to."

The conflict in his face seared her. She had lied to him about her identity and slept with him knowing he wouldn't have if he knew she was a Beaumont. And she was still lying. The enormity of her deception suddenly frightened her.

Gulping, Nina twisted out of his grasp. "It was bound to end anyway."

He stilled, and his expression grew enigmatic.

She should have left it at that, but maybe she was trying to justify her deception. "I mean, this thing between us, it was never going to develop into a full-on relationship. Right?"

His face turned rigid. "I'm not looking for a relationship."

The blunt reminder put her in her place. She was good enough for a brief fling, but not worthy of official girlfriend status. Well, maybe she deserved it for her lies.

Nina pressed her hands on the desk she was leaning against and forced herself to meet Joe's eyes. The prospect of not kissing Joe again, of not sharing the sweetest intimacies with him, left her feeling hollowed out and more than a little abandoned. That scared her. Joe had become an important part of her life so quickly. How had she let that happen?

"Maybe I should leave." The words jerked out of her.

"Leave?" He sounded bewildered.

"Yeah. Maybe I should find another job."

She had to return to San Francisco after the Food and Wine Festival anyway, and now Joe had given her a convenient out. Even though it hurt like crazy, this wake-up call was a relief. Now she had a good reason to leave Hartley, and he'd never know who she really was. Her guilty conscience festered at the continued subterfuge, but what good could come from confessing now? He'd never forgive her if he found out, but this way she could keep her memories of him and of this little town and all the people she'd met.

Joe's eyes were dark. "I don't want you to leave."

"But it's the best decision for both of us. I'll wait until after the festival."

He shook his head but said nothing, just stared bleakly at her.

She gulped, her throat raw. "We can still be friends while I'm here, can't we?"

"Friends." He heaved in a breath. "Yes. Friends."

"And I'm still going to help you at the B&B tomorrow. I want to," she added as he started to object. "You need all the help you can get." And maybe it would ease some of her remorse.

"Okay." He sighed as if in defeat. "Thanks. I'd better go now."

She stood stiffly to attention and watched as he opened the door.

"I'll see you out there." He tilted his head to indicate the public areas of the inn.

"See you there," she choked out.

Then he was gone.

. . .

Nina was relieved when Vince turned up on Monday to lend a hand. She and Joe had driven out to his B&B in awkward silence, and as soon as they'd arrived he had given her the task of clearing the gutters of the back porch, a one-man job, while he had quickly disappeared somewhere else.

He greeted Vince, and the two men started hammering something at the front of the house.

Nina, perched on a ladder, continued scooping out handfuls of dead leaves from the gutters. Restoring this mansion would be a huge task, but she could see it would make a fantastic B&B. Already she could visualize it in all its restored glory, a gracious, elegant residence that was also relaxed and comfortable. Her fantasies grew wilder and included Joe and herself, working together to bring the B&B to life.

She was so lost in her daydreams that it took her a while to notice the raised voices coming from the front of the house. She clambered down her ladder and hurried through the house. The front door stood wide-open, but when she saw who was outside, she skidded to a halt, her stomach diving.

Two men in black suits faced Joe and Vince. The man in charge, the one who stood in front with shades balanced on his head, was instantly recognizable to Nina. He was Perry Stevens, one of her father's smarmy, overambitious underlings, who made Nina's skin crawl.

And right now she could not let him see her.

She shrank back into an alcove beneath the staircase

from where she could still glimpse what was happening outside.

"Come on, Joe," Perry said in his usual oily manner. "It's a generous offer. You'll be able to pocket a handsome profit. All you have to do is sign this contract." He held out a sheaf of papers, a smirk on his face.

Joe stepped right up to him, rigid with fury, and thrust his head at Perry so that the smaller man faltered back. "The answer's still no. Do I have to tattoo that on your dumb forehead before Carson Beaumont gets the message?"

Perry tittered nervously. "Hey now, no need for that."

Joe grabbed the contract from Perry's fingers and stuffed it into the guy's jacket. "You have two minutes to get off my property."

"Maybe I'll come back when you're not so busy—"

"Yeah, come back any time and say hello to my shotgun." Joe jabbed his forefinger into Perry's chest, causing the man to stumble back. "Now get lost."

Face pale, Perry turned and signaled to the other man. The two revved off in a cloud of dust.

Nina pressed a hand to her mouth as she fought down nausea. She knew how her father operated. He'd tasked Perry to get Joe to sell, and Perry, always eager to suck up to her dad, would try just about anything. He was relentless, a Rottweiler who wouldn't let go once he'd clamped his jaws.

Joe and Vince were talking in low, tight voices, and before she could move they were in the hallway.

"Nina?" Vince approached her. "Did you hear all that?"

Nodding, she stepped out of the alcove. "I couldn't believe it. That was awful." Both men looked grim. She looked anxiously at Joe. "You don't really have a shotgun, do you?"

He shook his head, then sighed as he raked his hair, his frustration evident. "No, and I shouldn't have sunk to that, but those Beaumont jerks are feral."

And she had Beaumont blood flowing through her veins. She shivered with dread at the thought of being outed.

"Don't worry," Joe said, misinterpreting the reason for her distress. "I'm not going to do anything stupid."

Vince grunted. "Maybe you should think about getting a business partner."

"A business partner?" Joe raised his eyebrows at him.

"Yeah. If you can't get money from the banks, maybe you can find someone who wants to invest in your business."

"But I don't want someone else interfering in my plans."

Vince lifted his shoulders. "Maybe not, but at least you'd have a business, right? Anyway, it's something to think about." He walked off, leaving Nina alone with Joe.

"What do you think?" Joe asked her.

She couldn't answer for a moment. She was too busy thinking about her trust fund and how she would love to invest some of that money in Joe's venture. But of course she couldn't do that, not without revealing who she really was.

"I think it's worth considering," she said slowly.

He didn't speak, and the atmosphere became heavy and uncomfortable. His face was drawn, as if he hadn't slept well, and his dark eyes were enigmatic. But he was still Joe, and the hold he had over her was stronger than before. She longed to put her arms around him and comfort him. Wished she could bury her face in his chest and inhale his scent deep into her lungs. And when she caught the glimmer in his eyes, she knew he felt the same needs, the same regrets, and the same pain of denial.

"It'll be okay," Joe said.

She wasn't sure what he was referring to—the problems of his B&B or their broken affair—but she nodded anyway. Maybe Joe was right. Maybe everything would work out okay, though she couldn't see how.

Chapter Twelve

In the next few days, Nina had little time to brood as preparations for the Food and Wine Festival ramped up. Joe was busy with the organizing committee, while Sarah ruled the kitchen like a stressed kaiser, bawling out commands to her staff. The pressures on Joe must have been enormous, but he appeared to handle every minor and major crisis with aplomb, and she never once saw him lose his cool, though he must have wanted to at times.

She didn't see much of him, which was both good and bad. She missed his company. Missed his drop-dead handsomeness, and the flutter he gave her whenever she glimpsed him. But she also couldn't stop worrying about how her father threatened Joe's dreams and how Joe would react if he ever found out her true identity.

In an effort to distract her thoughts from Joe, she threw herself into her duties. The rooms at the Comet were immaculate as she polished every surface in sight and swept up every fleck of dirt. In the kitchen she volunteered for anything that needed doing and didn't mind Sarah's regular outbursts. She also found time to help Mrs. Stewart organize her stock for the charity stall. Her days passed in a blur of activity, and at night she fell into bed, exhausted. She didn't mind. She liked being part of the team, knowing she was making a contribution, however small, toward the success of the festival.

The festival began on Friday, and the crowds steadily built up over the weekend. Sarah's special menu was a hit, and the bar and restaurant did a roaring trade.

Saturday midmorning, Nina had just finished her cleaning duties and was heading out of the inn when Joe stopped her.

"Where're you hurrying off to?"

"It's my first shift at the charity stall. I don't want to be late."

"But you haven't had your break yet."

His brows drew together as he studied her in a way that made her self-conscious. She knew she didn't look her best. She hadn't been eating or sleeping well as each day ticked over and her departure drew closer and closer. She had asked Joe not to tell anyone she was leaving until the Monday after the festival. In fact, she planned to catch the early morning bus on Monday and be gone before anyone realized it. She hated good-byes, and the thought of having to say good-bye to Joe especially made her sick to the stomach.

"Did you have breakfast this morning?" Joe asked, still frowning.

She shook her head.

"Wait here," he said in a gentle yet commanding tone.

She waited, and a minute later he returned with something wrapped in a paper napkin.

"Here, eat this."

The savory tart in the napkin warmed her hands, and she found she had to blink back sudden tears. Tears because Joe had given her a tart?

"Thank you," she managed to say. This was the first exchange they'd had all week that wasn't about work. She had tried to avoid being alone with Joe, and she suspected he had done the same.

He shifted on his feet, pushing hands into pockets. "You gotta take care of yourself."

She battled the tears again. "You, too."

He was silent, and then someone came out, and the moment was over. Nina hurried off, slowly nibbling at the savory tart.

The beachside park where the main festival was set up was already buzzing with activity. There were stalls selling wine, cheese, sausages, and lavender. A jazz band played. A pancake-eating competition was about to start.

Mrs. Stewart greeted her warmly when she arrived at the stall. "Oh, am I glad to see you, dear. I've been run off my feet."

"Why don't you take a seat?" Nina suggested.

"You were right about those French dresses," Mrs. Stewart said with a smile as she sat down. "They've been flying off the racks."

Nina was delighted. "Oh, I'm so glad."

"We might have to go back to the store and pick up the rest." She waved to the throngs of people strolling around the park. "Can't disappoint our crowd."

"I didn't realize the festival would be so popular."

"It's all thanks to the organizing committee and

especially Joe. Hartley is a really nice little town. Not too big, not too small." Mrs. Stewart beamed with pride. "I've lived in plenty of other towns, but this is the only place where I've wanted to put down roots. What about you? You seem very settled here."

"Well, I don't know," Nina said, caught unawares by Mrs. Stewart's question.

A few weeks ago she would have definitely thought she wasn't cut out for small-town living, but now she wasn't so sure. She liked the people here, and people seemed to like her. The regulars at the Comet Inn, Mrs. Stewart and her charity workers, Vince, Joe's friends. They had all welcomed her. And none of them knew who she really was, so their friendliness had to be genuine. It would be nice to live here, to become a part of this community.

But that was never going to happen. Come Monday morning, she was leaving as suddenly as she'd arrived, and a month from now Hartley and all its residents, including Joe, would seem like a mirage to her.

And what would she be doing instead? She didn't know, but she did know that she wouldn't be working for her dad. How could she, knowing that he used attack dogs like Perry Stevens to bully people into submission? She didn't have much influence over her dad, but she'd use every ounce of it to make sure he backed off from Joe.

Sunday morning she dragged herself out of bed, her calf muscles already aching, and shuffled into the kitchen. She found Sarah preparing what seemed to be a mountain of spatchcocks.

"Hey," Sarah greeted Nina wearily. Her usually upright figure drooped, and there were deep shadows beneath her red-rimmed eyes.

Nina gaped at her. "Have you been here all night?"

The head chef shrugged. "I had a few hours' rest in my car."

"But that's insane. Does Joe know about this?"

Sarah instantly jerked her head up. "No, and don't you dare tell him." She glared at Nina with her usual pepper. "The kitchen is my domain, no one else's."

"Still, you could have asked for help." Nina filled a kettle and switched it on before hauling out a coffee press. "You want some coffee?"

"That'd be great." A trace of appreciation flickered across Sarah's face.

Nina made the coffee, filled two mugs, and passed one to Sarah. After a few reviving gulps, Nina set down the mug and dusted her hands. "Tell me what I can do to help."

"Well, you could chop up walnuts and parsley. That way Chris can help me with the spatchcock when he comes in. But you need to pay attention to your work. The walnuts and parsley have to be evenly cut. No lumpy bits."

Nina spent several hours helping Sarah prep. She went upstairs to clean the rooms, then did another shift at the charity stall before returning to the inn. By then the lunch crowds were beginning to thicken, and the next couple of hours passed in hectic activity. The pace had slowed to a trickle when Sarah grabbed Nina by the elbow and almost frog-marched her out the back.

"I just wanted to say thanks for all your help this week-end." Sarah crossed her arms, frowning and looking uncomfortable. "I appreciate your help."

Nina waved her hand. "It was nothing."

"No, it wasn't nothing." The furrows on Sarah's brow deepened, and she pulled at her lower lip. "We, uh, we got off on the wrong foot initially. I was convinced you wouldn't last. Also, to be honest, I thought you were bad news for Joe."

"I wouldn't do anything to hurt Joe." Nina's throat tightened, and she couldn't help adding, "Joe's a great guy."

The other woman looked away as she shuffled her Doc Martens in the loose gravel. "Yeah, he is." There was a long pause before she sighed. "I guess I'm defensive about Joe because I used to have a thing for him."

Dumbfounded, Nina turned her gasp into a cough. "Oh, really?" she spluttered.

Sarah's face had turned a deep red. "I'm over it now, but it took me a while." She shook her head. "For years I held a candle for the guy and did nothing about it. *You* wouldn't be so useless."

"Me?"

"Yes, you. You're the type who wouldn't hold back. You'd tell Joe exactly how you feel, then you'd probably drag him into bed, too."

A hot tide engulfed Nina's face. God, if Sarah knew what she and Joe had been up to… But it was over now, she was leaving tomorrow, and she'd hate to damage Joe's relationship with Sarah.

Wiping her hands on her apron, she backed away a few steps. "You've got the wrong idea about me, Sarah. When it comes to men, I'm as clueless as the next girl. And I'm glad you're over Joe."

"Like I said, it took a while." Sarah's lips pulled down. "But I'm fine now. Joe's a great boss, and I love cooking here. I'm glad I didn't screw that up or I'd be left with nothing."

Nina's stomach contracted. *She* had screwed up royally, and now *she* was left with nothing. Suddenly she couldn't bear any further confessions from Sarah.

Nina slipped back into the inn and hurried to the bathroom near her room, where she splashed cold water over her face. After a few deep breaths to calm herself, she left. She was walking past Joe's office when he called out to her, and every nerve ending in her body jumped in response.

He rose from his desk as she entered. "I wanted to say thanks for all your hard work this weekend, especially in the kitchen." He rounded his desk to stand in front of her. "I know Sarah can be a hard-ass, so I'm glad you don't hold it against her."

"Uh, thanks."

"I mean it, Nina. And it's not just me. Everyone here appreciates the effort you put into it."

She couldn't help flushing at his praise. "Yeah, well, guess I don't break as many plates now."

"This is a tough mob to impress. I'm tough to impress. You've earned our respect."

She could tell he meant every word. She *had* earned their respect, and she'd done it without her name or wealth to confuse the situation. This respect was all hers. She'd achieved the goal she'd set for herself when she'd first wandered into Hartley, and nothing could take that away from her.

"Thanks." It was something to remember when she was far away from Joe.

He rubbed his hands against his jeans. "I'll miss you when you're gone."

She gaped at him. Her eyelids began to twitch, and she couldn't help sniffing.

"Nina? Are you okay?"

No, she wanted to shout. *I am not okay!* This time tomorrow she would be miles away from him, and she'd never see him again. In what universe could that be okay? Her chest heaved, and to her horror her lower lip started to tremble.

"Nina…" He touched her shoulder, and even through her turmoil she registered that his hand shook. "Maybe… you don't want to go?"

But she had to. She *had* to. Her heart twisted and turned like a captive bird desperate to find an escape.

She could only stay if she told Joe the truth. But if she did that, he wouldn't want her to stay… Or would he? It was a high-risk gamble with awful odds. Even if she told Joe who she was and, by some miracle, he forgave her the deception, he wasn't offering her a relationship. He'd never wanted a relationship.

Joe's fingers tightened on her shoulder, and she saw the strain in his eyes. Maybe Joe was slowly realizing that he didn't want to be a bachelor all his life. Maybe he could envision some sort of future…with her?

She licked her lips, dizzy with fear and hope and tiredness. The choices before her were so scary she could hardly think straight.

"Nina?" A male voice spoke from the door behind her. "Is that you?"

The confusion in her head shattered and reformed into black dread.

No, it can't be… She spun round to find her worst fears confirmed—her father stood in the open doorway.

Whether she wanted him to or not, Joe was about to find out who she really was.

Chapter Thirteen

"Dad!" Her voice was a high-pitched squeak. "What on earth are you doing here? How—how did you find me?"

Carson Beaumont stepped into the room, his face craggy with disapproval. "I got it out of Lindsey."

Lindsey! How could her best friend have given her up? But Nina knew what a bulldozer her father could be when he wanted something. Lindsey had probably tried calling to warn her, but Nina's cell phone lay forgotten in her room.

"Dad, I don't—"

"Are you the owner of this place?" Her father's suspicious gaze had moved past her and fixed on Joe.

"That's right," Joe said stiffly, holding out his hand. "Joe Farina."

Her father ignored Joe's outstretched hand and turned back to Nina. "What the hell are you doing in a place like this? I thought you were taking a vacation, but—" He pulled a face as he waved at her grubby jeans and work-soiled

T-shirt. "It sure doesn't look like it, from the way you're dressed."

She flushed with anger at his rudeness toward Joe, toward herself. But before she could speak, Joe interrupted.

"Nina's not a guest here," Joe snapped, his face tight with anger. "She's my maid and busgirl."

Carson's jaw sagged open. "You mean to say she's…"

"Yup. Your daughter is scrubbing toilets, clearing tables, washing dishes. She even peels vegetables on occasion."

"You've got to be kidding me." Her father gaped at Nina, completely bewildered. "*Why?*"

A hot lump in her throat prevented her from breathing. The sound of impending doom crashed in her brain.

"Dad, we need to talk."

"Damn straight we do. You've got a lot of explaining to do, young lady."

Finally anger spurted out, a welcome relief. "Don't treat me like a child. We're going to talk as adults and equals, or not at all."

Her father blinked at her in surprise. "Fine. But you're going to tell me everything."

Joe moved between them, his eyes flinty. "Maybe you'd like to talk here in my study, Mr. Summers," Joe said, his voice like steel.

"Summers? My name's not Summers." He appeared offended that he wasn't instantly recognizable. "I'm Carson Beaumont," he announced in that booming, self-important tone of his that made Nina wince.

She couldn't breathe again. She could only watch as sheer disbelief blanked out Joe's expression.

"Carson Beaumont?" he echoed, incredulous. "The guy

who's been trying to get his grubby hands on my property so he can bulldoze it and dump a fucking megaresort here? The guy who sends his numbskull goons to do his dirty work for him? *That* Carson Beaumont?" His face puckered with disgust.

Nina's father puffed up with rage. "Who the hell are— Wait a minute! I thought this town rang a bell, and now I remember who you are—"

"That's right, I'm the owner of that property you're so desperate to buy," Joe snarled. "And I'm *never* going to sell to you."

"Now don't be so hasty." Carson adjusted the collar of his jacket, looking highly annoyed. "Damn that Perry. Can't rely on him to do a simple job."

Joe turned on Nina, his eyes blazing with fury. "You're Carson Beaumont's daughter? I can't believe it." His contempt made her skin peel.

"Please, I can explain." She reached for him, but he jerked away like she was contaminated.

"I don't want to hear it."

Without another word, he exited the room, leaving behind an emotional vacuum that threatened to burst Nina's chest.

"That fella needs a lesson in manners," her father grouched.

Helpless fury filled her. "Look who's talking! You refused to shake hands with him!" Her entire body was shaking with shock.

Carson screwed up his forehead. "What's got into you?"

She couldn't do this in Joe's office. "Let's go somewhere else," she said and led the way next door to her room.

"What's this?" Her father looked about the bare room,

his nose wrinkling. "Don't tell me this is where you've been sleeping?"

She huffed impatiently. "It's fine, Dad."

He clasped her arm. "Tell me the truth. Are you okay? Did Farina do anything to you, because if he's hurt you, I swear I'll make him pay."

"Never mind that," she snapped. "Why the hell are you trying to squeeze Joe into selling his property to you? Why can't you leave him alone?" Her cheeks were hot with anger, and she was having trouble controlling her temper.

He waved a hand dismissively. "It's just business—"

"Business? I knew you were a hard-ass, but I never thought you could be so ruthless. I'm ashamed of you."

His eyes hardened. "Where do you think the money comes from to buy you BMWs?"

"Oh, no. Don't try to put the blame on me. You do this all for yourself. You enjoy stomping over other people. Well, not this time. You're not going to stomp over Joe and this town."

Her father blinked and stared at her as if seeing her for the first time.

"Does this Farina guy have something over you? Is he forcing you to work here without telling anyone?"

She sighed in exasperation. Her father wasn't going to give ground on his business dealings with Joe, and neither was she, but that battle would have to wait until later.

"He didn't force me to do anything. This job was all my idea."

"But why? I don't understand? You *want* a crap job in the boondocks?" Her father looked almost comical in his amazement. "And why did you give him a false name?"

"I didn't want anyone here to know who I was. I wanted to forget I was a Beaumont, at least for a while."

"By cleaning toilets and busing tables? People like us don't do that."

"Don't be such a snob. Someone has to do those jobs, so why not me?"

"Because you have several million reasons not to."

"Oh, why don't you see?" She whirled on him. "I'm sick of being a Beaumont. That name and that money ruin everything!"

Carson looked taken aback. "You're still hurting over Oliver. I can understand that. I never took him for a fortune hunter either."

Nina shook her head. "It's more than Oliver; it's my job, too. My manager gave me a promotion, but everyone I work with thinks I only got it because I'm a Beaumont, and when I talked to Harry about it, he sounded so weird I knew something was up. Did you order him to promote me?"

He lifted his hands. "Not ordered, encouraged. And I was only trying to help you."

"Then why don't you let me win or lose on my own merits?" She fumed at him, incredulous that her father could be so dense at times. "What on earth possessed you to do that?"

"Because I want you to stay at the company," he blustered, looking irritated. "You pulled some crazy stunts when you were younger, and look! You're still pulling crazy stunts. Who in their right mind runs away to be a maid? And without even telling anyone?" He thrust his hands upward. "No one but you, Nina. I was right to chase you down. I mean, how long were you planning on hanging around here anyway?"

"I was going to come home tomorrow." She huffed. "I wasn't running away for good. I knew I had to get back to my job." The job she didn't want anymore. But that argument, too, could wait for another day.

Carson grunted. "If that's the case, I'm getting you out of this place right now. The helicopter is waiting at the airfield. We can be gone as soon as you've packed your things." He made a face at her working gear. "Although, if that's what you're wearing these days, you might as well leave everything behind. You can restock your wardrobe back in San Francisco."

Alarm heaved in her stomach. She wasn't ready for this. She'd been gearing up to slink out tomorrow morning, but she wasn't prepared to leave right this second. "Um, you flew here in the helicopter?" she asked, stalling for time.

"Yes. I don't have all day."

Of course he didn't, and with the helicopter emblazoned with his company name, everyone in town would know by now he'd arrived. Nina's heart sank at the thought of the whole town figuring who she really was.

Her dad moved toward the door. "You drove here, didn't you? I'll get someone to drive your Beemer down to San Francisco."

"Actually, I'm going to need someone with a crane or something. I had a little accident. The car sank into the water in a disused quarry."

"What!"

"I'm really sorry."

He grumped something that sounded like "more crazy stunts," and this time she couldn't blame him.

"I'll take care of the car," she said, and when he went to

protest, she added, "No, really. It's my car and my responsi-bility. I'll handle it."

"Fine." He flicked at his jacket sleeve. "Can we go now?"

Her mouth dried. "I want to talk to Joe first. Alone. Can you wait out in the bar or something?"

He heaved a sigh of resignation. "I'll wait in the hired car. It's a black Merc outside. Don't take too long. Ellen and I have a party to attend this evening."

He stomped out of the room, leaving Nina shaken and tense. Not because of what had just happened, but because of what was yet to happen. Between her and Joe. She need-ed to see him one last time, even knowing that he despised her. Despite whatever fury he threw at her, she owed him an explanation.

• • •

Joe stood in the hallway outside Nina's room, his body raging with a strange, desperate anger. As soon as he'd seen Carson Beaumont leave the inn, he'd strode back here to wait. To wait for Nina and the showdown they had to have.

The door opened, and Nina stopped dead as their gazes clashed. His stomach snarled. He motioned with his head for her to follow him. Mistrust and fury pounded against his skull as he marched into his office, waited for her to enter, and shut the door.

"Did your father put you up to this?" he barked out. His tension had reached the breaking point.

"What? No." She shook her head in bewilderment.

"Don't act dumb. You lied your way into a job here so you could spy on me and tell your father everything I was doing."

Her jaw sagged. "That's not true! My dad didn't know I was here."

He barely heard her as nasty suspicions poisoned his mind. "Did he really expect you to sleep with me? Or was that just a little extra fun for you?"

Her face paled. "If what you say is true, why would my dad drop in like he did and blow my cover, huh?"

Maybe that part at least was true. He blinked and looked at her with fresh, cynical eyes. "Jesus Christ. I still can't believe you're his daughter. Annette Martha Beaumont. Yeah, I looked you up on the internet while you were powwowing with your dad. Your sister is marrying a senator's son. That's the wedding you were talking about." He shook his head in disbelief. "You've been lying to me since the day we met."

"Joe, I'm so sorry for lying." She lowered her head as if ashamed. "You don't know how sorry."

"I'll bet." He couldn't stop staring at her. She was Carson Beaumont's daughter, for Christ's sakes. He'd given her orders, reprimanded her, worked with her, ate with her, slept with her. Goddammit.

"I am sorry, truly, but I had my reasons. I lied about my name and my background because I wanted to get away from them. I was tired of the way my name or my money always ruined my life."

Joe snorted. "Yeah, it's so hard when your daddy's a billionaire. I suppose you've got a nice little trust fund of your own just in case."

She bit her lip. "Yes, I have a trust fund from my mother's will."

"How much?" he couldn't help asking.

"Fifteen million."

Sweet Jesus. Fifteen million dollars, and he had bought her sneakers, for crying out loud! Had she secretly laughed at him? Had she enjoyed duping him and everyone else? Maybe she wasn't sorry about the lies, only about being caught.

Her big blue eyes were fixed on him, filled with what seemed to be trepidation, and despite everything he wanted to pull her into his arms and comfort her. Hell, what was wrong with him? Why couldn't he despise her the way he should?

"Oh, aren't you the poor little rich girl," he burst out, tormented by his angry confusion. "Can't think what to do with your fifteen million? Or maybe you were worried I'd touch you for a loan? Is that why you didn't tell me?"

Her cheeks flushed with indignation. "I didn't tell you because I knew it would affect the way you treat me."

"Damn right it does."

"And that just proves my point. You're no better than— than my ex-boyfriend! He was only with me because I'm rich, and now you're letting my money affect the way you think of me."

"You're wrong. It's not your money or your name I object to, but your lies." He jabbed a finger at her. "You knew your father was trying to strong-arm me into selling my B&B, and yet you didn't say a thing."

She jabbed a finger back at him. "Oh, yes, I'm sure you'd have been so understanding if I'd said, 'Oh, by the way, that billionaire you're having trouble with? He's my dad.' Yeah, right."

Resentment flared as he recalled how Nina's father had

harassed and tormented him all these months. "Well, you can tell your billionaire daddy that I would rather be eaten alive by ants than sell to him. He is never getting his hands on my property."

She sucked in a breath as if he'd hit her, and for a moment he regretted his harsh words, but she quickly recovered and aimed a chilly glare at him. "I thought you were different, Joe, but you're just like all the other phonies I've had to deal with in my life. I'll give your message to my father. He's waiting for me outside."

Her dignity pierced him, but his anger was black and choking. Nina had deceived him and continued the deception after they became lovers and after she knew what her father was doing to him. How could he forgive her for that? And how could he forgive himself for still wanting her? That was the worst part, this humiliating hold she had over him, this desire to embrace her and kiss her until the outside world went away. It was infuriating, degrading, unbearable.

"I thought you were different, too." The words ground out of his clamped lips. He stared at her a moment longer. Then he turned abruptly and left.

. . .

Nina waited a few seconds before her shoulders slumped and she had to clutch at the desk to stop herself from collapsing. Now she knew the truth. Joe cared more for his property than he did for her. Everything else was forgotten, not just the amazing sex, but the tender friendship that had sprung up between them. Her help at his B&B, her visiting his nonna with him, the conversations they'd had. None of that was worth remembering.

He only saw that she was a Beaumont, and therefore someone he despised.

Her body heaved biliously. She shut her eyes to fight the nausea. When she opened them, Vince was standing in the doorway.

Her heart sank even further. Oh, no, she couldn't withstand another confrontation.

"Vince, I…"

He shook his head. "You don't have to explain. I know who you are. Joe couldn't help blurting it out earlier, and your father isn't exactly inconspicuous. There's a crowd building out there. I thought you might need some help."

His unwarranted kindness brought tears back to her eyes. "But why are you…?"

He took her arm gently. "You're a good person, Nina."

Tears spilled over and ran down her cheeks. "Joe doesn't think so," she choked out.

"Give him time. We'd better go now, or your father will come stomping in again."

Vince guided her out. The lobby was busy, people coming and going, but everyone paused to stare at her. Vince kept her going, his hand firm on her elbow, and she'd never been so grateful. There was no sign of Sarah. Or Joe. But she didn't expect to see Joe again.

Outside the Comet Inn, the afternoon sunshine almost blinded her. Someone opened a car door for her, and Vince guided her into the backseat.

"Thank you," she said weakly to Vince.

He didn't reply, just squeezed her hand before letting her go. Then the door slammed and the car zoomed off and she was alone with her father.

Thankfully, he was still busy on his cell phone. "Yes, Ellen, we're on our way home now. Thank God. I can't wait to get out of Hicksville."

Nina rolled herself into a ball and squeezed herself into the far corner. She'd stopped crying, but an ocean of tears was gathering inside her, and sometime soon she would have to let them flow. But not yet.

Chapter Fourteen

On Monday morning Nina swept into her father's office, high on the twenty-first floor of a skyscraper overlooking downtown San Francisco. She didn't have an appointment, but the personal assistant didn't try to stop her, probably cowed by the thunderous expression on her face.

Wearing a gray shift dress and black ankle boots, her blonde hair slicked back, Nina was dressed for business, and she detected a flicker of wary surprise in her father's face as he rose to greet her.

"I didn't expect to see you here today," he said, gesturing to a visitor's chair. "Thought you'd want some time off to recover from your…experience. In fact, why don't you take a couple of days off? I'm sure your manager won't mind."

Nina remained standing and unsmiling. "I said I'd be back at work today, and I am."

"Yes, but…" Carson seemed uncertain for once. He cleared his throat. "So, what can I do for you?"

She drew in a breath. This was going to be difficult, but she was determined to see it through. Not just for herself, but for Joe, and the others in Hartley. "I came to tell you a number of things. First of all, I'm resigning."

"Resigning? You just got promoted."

How could her father be so dense? "I don't want to work for a company where people aren't promoted on merit."

He had the grace to blush, but only faintly. "All right, I admit that was clumsy of me. But look, I've thought of a solution. Wait till you hear this."

Nina suppressed a groan. Whatever he had up his sleeve, she wasn't interested. She couldn't work for her father anymore. Not on any terms.

He didn't seem to notice her reluctance. "I just picked up an old resort in Palm Springs. It used to be popular, but now it's run-down. The staff are so behind the times they're practically prehistoric, but they're all unionized, so they can't all be fired without inviting more trouble. The trick is to bring in new work practices without alienating too many people. It's a tricky job, but if you took it on and did it well, no one could accuse you of not pulling your weight. And I promise not to interfere." Carson spread his hands wide. "What do you say, Nina?"

"No, Dad." She sighed. "I appreciate the offer, but I can't work for you. Not when some of your business practices are so appalling. Which brings me to my second decision." She sucked in her stomach and squared her chin, ready to do battle. "I want you to back off Joe. I want you to leave him alone and stop putting pressure on him to sell his property."

Her father's conciliatory manner evaporated. He walked away from her and resumed his throne-like chair behind his oversize desk.

"I can't agree to that. Business is business, and I can't let you change my plans on a whim." He spoke patronizingly at her, as if she were a child. "You don't need to worry. Everything we do is aboveboard."

Her blood boiled as she stalked up to his desk and leaned her hands against it. "Aboveboard, my ass. You sent that grubby tapeworm Perry Stevens to threaten Joe. To use Joe's sick grandmother against him. And when that didn't work, Perry went to the local banks and whispered in their ears not to lend Joe the money he needs." She bent over the desk to glare at her father. "How is any of that aboveboard? It's sickening, and I'm ashamed to be related to you."

"I didn't tell Perry to go that far," Carson protested.

"Oh, please. Are you saying weaselly Perry did all that by himself?"

"I told him to be tough, but I never told him to go to any banks or snoop around sick grandmothers. Sometimes Perry's too smart by half."

Nina crossed her arms, trying to gauge if he was being honest. "Are you telling the truth?"

"Of course I am. I play hard, but I don't go below the belt. I have a reputation to uphold."

And that was more important than her opinion of him, obviously. Her heart dipped, but she decided that his reasons didn't matter as long as Joe was protected.

"So you'll leave Joe alone?" she asked, hope rising.

"I'll yank Perry back," Carson said grimly. "But I can't promise to leave Farina alone. I want my resort, and it can't happen without his property."

His determined words crushed her hopes. "Build your

resort somewhere else." She scowled at him.

"I want it there." He scowled back at her before a calculating look entered his eyes. "Maybe there's a compromise we can both agree on."

"What?"

"I'll back off your precious Joe if you take the job in Palm Springs."

She clamped her lips and thought through the implications. She hated the idea of going to Palm Springs and working for her father. But if it helped Joe, then wouldn't it be worth it?

Yes. She would do it. She would do it for Joe even though he despised her. She would do it to make amends for her lies, but mostly because Joe deserved it. Because he was good and honest and wonderful. Because…her heart shuddered as the stark truth overwhelmed her. Because she *loved* Joe. She loved him, and she'd do anything for him. Even if he never knew, even if she never saw him again. Pain rippled through her, but it was a pain she welcomed. Finally, she knew what real love was like. Real love hurt, but it also inspired her. Made her a better, stronger person.

"Nina? What's wrong?"

She blinked away the tears that threatened to spill out. "Nothing. I'm just thinking about Palm Springs."

"So you agree?"

"Yes." Maybe moving to the desert might stop her from moping too much.

Her father sighed, looking strangely relieved. "All right, then. It's a deal." He held out his hand to her.

They shook hands, and they both sat.

"Happy now?" her father asked.

She shrugged. She doubted she'd ever be happy again, not the way Joe made her happy. But at least Joe would get his dream, and *he* could be happy.

"Seems like a poor deal from your perspective," she said. "You're giving up a multimillion-dollar resort, and all you're getting in return is me working in Palm Springs." She peered at him, a little suspicious. "Why are you so eager for me to stay?"

"Because I want to protect you. Because I haven't always been there for you in the past, and I want to make it up to you." He paused and scratched at his neck, looking uncomfortable.

Nina's mouth fell open. "Oh."

He waved a hand, still discomfited. "I know I haven't always been the best dad, especially after your mom died and I married Ellen and brought her and Brooke into your life. I know you didn't like that."

"Oh, God, Dad," Nina exclaimed. "I don't resent you for marrying Ellen. I didn't want you to be alone for the rest of your life, and neither did Mom. She wanted you to be happy." It felt strange to talk about her mom with him, since they'd rarely done so in the past.

He swiped a hand over his forehead. "But you were always acting out, doing crazy things."

To get his attention. But that was water under the bridge. "Guess I'm just a regular pain in the ass."

"Your mom knew how to handle you, whereas I never could. Didn't want all the hassle, I suppose. But when you got arrested over that protest, I knew I had to do something. I thought giving you a job in the company was the best way to keep tabs on you." He sighed, and he seemed softer, kinder, more fatherly than he'd ever been. "I'm glad we're on the same page now. You're going to do great in Palm Springs. Who knows, maybe one day you'll be running this business."

"I seriously doubt that." Feeling worn-out, Nina rose to go.

"But you're my daughter," he called after her. "Business runs in your blood."

"Talk to you later, Dad." She made her escape.

The only business she'd be interested in running would be something she had a hand in creating. Unbidden, an image of Joe's B&B, restored to gleaming elegance, drifted into her mind, before bleakness chilled her. Joe would get his dream, but she'd have no part in it. She would have to find her own dream, without Joe, but that seemed impossible.

• • •

Joe flipped open his laptop in his office. It was Wednesday, and he still hadn't tallied up his profits from the festival. It was unusually tardy for him, but after staring at the screen for half an hour, he'd made no progress and almost welcomed the interruption when Sarah appeared at his side holding a plate of food.

"I thought you could do with some lunch." She slid the plate of sizzling garlic prawns onto his desk.

He'd had two cups of coffee for breakfast and nothing since then. The prawns were plump and juicy but didn't stir his appetite.

"Thanks, but I'm not hungry. You have them."

Sighing, she sat down and forked up a prawn. "I'll make you a tuna sandwich for later."

"Why are you making me lunch anyway?"

She shrugged. "Just trying to be helpful."

"Yeah? What makes you think I need help?" Joe blew out a breath. Ever since Sunday he'd noticed both Vince and Sarah treating him like a kid who'd just had a tonsillectomy.

Sarah toyed with her fork. "Um, well, you've been working long hours this week."

"So? I always work long hours."

"Yes, but usually you're not so…" She hesitated then dropped her fork with a clatter. "Look, we're worried about you. Ever since Nina left you've been…moody."

Joe scowled. "I'm not *pining* for her, if that's what you think." He shook with indignation.

"You're not?"

Christ, what else had Sarah and Vince noticed about him? "Definitely not." He jabbed a finger at his laptop. "If you don't mind, I've got work to finish here before I visit my nonna this afternoon."

Grimacing, Sarah gripped the plate in front of her. "You know, sometimes I think you use your work and your grandmother as an excuse not to get involved."

He gaped at her. "What the hell are you talking about?"

She leaned forward, her expression earnest. "I know about the girl who cheated on you when your grandma was injured. Ever since then you've closed yourself off from relationships, telling everyone, including yourself, that you're too busy with your work, your grandmother, your town duties, your whatever. But that's just a convenient way of avoiding getting hurt again, isn't it?"

Joe struggled to breathe. Was this really Sarah, his tough, no-nonsense chef, giving him romantic advice?

Before he could formulate a coherent answer, Sarah continued, "I think you really feel something for Nina, but you're too scared to admit it to yourself."

A bitter laugh burst from him. "Nina? Have you forgotten all her lies? Have you forgotten she's Carson Beaumont's *daughter*?"

"I know she lied, but she worked hard—even I can admit that. I figure she had good reasons for concealing her identity."

Oh, this was too much. Joe made a slicing gesture with his hand. "Whoever she is, I've forgotten all about her."

"You wouldn't be so angry if you weren't in love with her."

Joe gulped. He wasn't in love with Nina. He wasn't. He was only angry because she'd fooled him.

He repeated the words like a mantra.

Sarah was looking wistful. "Hey, I've been there, you know…had feelings for someone who didn't return them." She prodded at the prawns. "But I think Nina has a thing for you, too. A ginormous thing. You should tell her how you feel."

No. Way. In. Hell.

He pushed to his feet. "I've got to go."

He hotfooted it out of his study. Someone was coming down the hall. He turned and stomped blindly into the next room, only to realize his mistake—he'd walked into Nina's old room. Someone had stripped the bed and left Nina's clothes neatly folded on the mattress. Beneath the bed her turquoise Crocs were neatly lined up.

The sight of those Crocs made his heart spasm with pain. Leaning against the door for support, he squeezed his eyes shut. Was he never going to forget about Nina?

· · ·

Saturday morning Joe woke up early after another sleepless night and drove to his B&B. But his heart wasn't into it, and he wondered if he had the necessary energy to see this project through. Each time he came here he was reminded of Nina and how she'd helped him so enthusiastically. She'd shared his vision for this place, and now he couldn't be here without thinking of her.

It was the same at his home or at the inn. Nina had wormed her way into his life so effectively it seemed he'd never be able to forget her.

A knock on the door was a welcome distraction, and he greeted Vince with relief. Maybe his friend could take his mind off Nina.

But Vince disappointed him. They had just started ripping some rampant ivy away from the outer walls when Vince said conversationally, "So have you spoken to Nina recently?"

Joe's back cramped up. "No, why would I?" he retorted.

Vince gave a mild shrug. "Just thought after a week you'd have calmed down and gotten your head straight about her."

"What's that supposed to mean?"

"I understand why you got so mad when you found out who she was, but, well, she's still Nina. She's still the same person you fell for." Vince's eyes were trained on him. "Isn't she?"

Despite the cool morning air, Joe suddenly felt hot and uncomfortable. Six nights of sleepless tossing. Six days of feverish arguments and counterarguments. He couldn't go on like this.

He grabbed hold of a thick vine and yanked at it viciously. "I don't know anything anymore, man." He tore off a chunk of ivy. "Except one thing. I can't for the fucking life of me stop thinking about her."

Vince nodded. "Knew you had it bad."

His bare hands were smarting. He scowled at his friend. "Is that all you got for me?"

"Nope. I think you should go talk to her."

"Talk to her? You mean…drive down to San Francisco to see her?" The idea seemed outrageous.

"That's the general idea." Vince grinned.

"But—" Joe's head started to spin. "What would I say?"

"I dunno. Maybe you should just tell her you love her. I hear chicks go for that."

Joe wanted to strangle his friend. "Yeah, that's a big help, Vince!" He hurled away the mangled bit of ivy. His heart hammered in his chest like an engine about to explode, while his brain churned out frightening scenarios of baring his soul to Nina.

"Okay, so I don't know exactly what you'd say to her, but you'd think of something, I'm sure. And anything is better than galumphing around like the Hunchback of Notre Dame."

Joe let out a seething hiss. He dug his fingers into his brow, desperately trying to order his thoughts. "I don't even know where she lives."

"That's okay. I read on the internet that Beaumont's daughter Brooke is getting married today at the Beaumonts' home in Presidio Heights. I can text you the address."

"And you think they'll just let me walk in off the street, huh?"

Vince rubbed his jaw, considering. "Well, you might want to take a shower before you go. I hear chicks like that, too." He held up his hands as Joe growled at him. "Hey, are you going to let a little wedding invitation stand in your way? Just tell them you're her plus one and bluff your way in."

I must be going crazy, Joe thought, because he was actually contemplating how long it would take him to get to San Francisco. And excitement was bubbling in him at the prospect of seeing Nina again. Excitement and fear and doubt. He needed to see her again. Just one more time without all the anger clouding his brain. He needed her, just plain needed her, which meant...

"Aw, damn," he muttered as prickling chills raced up and down his spine.

"What?" Vince asked.

"I do love her, you know. I just didn't realize it until now."

Vince clapped him on the shoulder. "Save it for Nina, buddy. Doesn't work on me."

Chapter Fifteen

The devil had reserved a special dose of hell for those attending a wedding with a broken heart, and Nina had felt the flames licking her all afternoon. It didn't help that the wedding was an overblown extravaganza and the guest list was stuffed with socialites, politicians, business execs, and all the other people Nina had so little in common with. For hours she pretended she was having a good time until Brooke and the senator's son finally left, bound for their honeymoon by private jet.

Nina had talked Lindsey into coming to the wedding as her guest, and they found a quiet table to themselves. Nina had gotten hold of a bottle of expensive wine, with every intention of getting hammered, but now it didn't seem worth the effort. Everything felt like hard work these days. She felt so flat and empty and…old.

"You really think moving to Palm Springs is a good idea?" Lindsey asked, sipping her wine.

"I told you why I'm doing it."

"Yes, but Joe doesn't even know you're doing it for him."

"It's okay. As long as he's happy." She clenched her jaw against the pain.

Lindsey squeezed Nina's hand. "He's a dope and doesn't deserve your sacrifice."

"It doesn't matter. It's done." Nina let out a sigh. "Tomorrow I'm leaving for Palm Springs, and I start my new job on Monday." She tried to inject some energy into her voice. "It'll be good having something to keep me busy."

Lindsey wrinkled her nose. "I'm worried about you, Nina. You're not your usual self."

How could she be her usual self when she was in love with Joe? When she was trying so hard to get over him?

"I'm just tired."

She tried to imagine Joe at this wedding reception. What would he make of all this conspicuous consumption? The rivers of French champagne, the masses of hothouse flowers, the fortunes dangling on necks and wrists? He wouldn't be out of place, she decided. Because Joe was his own man. He was strong and independent. He wasn't defined by what he owned.

The band had started playing a croony number, and on the dance floor couples were snuggling up to each other. Nina shuddered. She'd had enough happy couples for one day.

She hauled herself to her feet. "Do you want to hang around here? Because I'm done."

"Let's go, then," Lindsey said softly.

"Let's take the back way and avoid the crowds."

As they made their way toward the rear, Nina heard

a small commotion coming from the main entrance. *Just some drunk*, she thought. *You can't have a wedding without someone getting sloshed.*

. . .

Joe was in a fury. It hadn't helped that his truck had sprung a punctured tire halfway to San Francisco. Changing the tire had gotten him sweaty and messy. He'd gone to such care making himself presentable, and then ended up with wrinkled pants, grease stains on his shirt, and his hair all disheveled. He wasn't usually so clumsy, but the prospect of seeing Nina again had put him into a tailspin.

So much so that once he'd reached the city he'd quickly gotten lost. The GPS on his phone couldn't pick up a signal, and he'd spent ages driving blind until he got his bearings and found the Beaumont residence in the prestigious Presidio Heights suburb. It looked like the fanciest house in the street, a three-story mansion surrounded by a huge garden and massive walls and gates manned by security guards.

Lights blazed in the garden while music and chatter rose up in the night air. It was getting late, and some of the wedding guests were leaving, judging by the Bentleys and Mercs edging in and out of the grounds.

This activity abetted his party crashing. With valet drivers and cars milling around, the lone security guard at the gate was distracted. Possibly he also wasn't expecting anyone to crash the wedding at this late hour. Joe took his chance and calmly strolled through the gates as if he had every right to be there.

He stood for a moment, taking in the impressive mansion

and sweeping grounds. So this was where Nina had grown up. It seemed incredible that a girl from this background had been his maid. His respect for her rose even higher, and he realized he didn't care that Carson was her father, because Nina was clearly her own woman. His anxiety to see her intensified.

He made for the giant tent set up in the middle of the garden, where all the light and noise was coming from. His heartbeat climbed as he straightened his shirt and rehearsed the first lines he'd say to Nina.

What if she refused to see him? What if she had him thrown out? Sweat prickled his nape. Hell, he couldn't think about that.

He paused at the entrance to the tent, momentarily dazed by the lights and music. Several guests peered at him. The men were in tuxedos, the women dripping with jewels. They looked at him as if they couldn't decide whether he was part of the waitstaff or some weird cousin from out of town.

"Hey!" someone yelled out. "What the hell are you doing here?"

Joe turned to see Perry Stevens scurrying up. *Oh, great. Just what I need right now.*

"I'm with Nina," Joe said coolly.

Perry gawked at him. "Nina? Mr. Beaumont's daughter?" He let out a cackle. "Oh, that's priceless."

Ignoring the twerp, Joe scanned the crowd, searching for a slim figure with a mop of short blonde hair. He couldn't see her. He moved forward, intent on searching every inch.

Someone grabbed his arm. "Where the hell do you think you're going?"

He glanced down at Perry's sweaty, flushed face. The guy looked drunk and ugly. In a sudden rush of revulsion, Joe shook him off. Perry stumbled back, then he lurched toward Joe, fists swinging wildly. Joe stuck out one hand, palm flattened, and the guy bounced off and landed on his ass.

People were gathering around, murmurs were flying. Perry scrambled upright, face puce as he started to screech. "Security! Security! This man assaulted me. Security!"

Joe groaned silently. This was so not the way he'd envisioned meeting Nina again. He hadn't thought this through. He'd allowed Vince to convince him that crashing a wedding to plead with the woman he loved was a smart idea.

"Perry, for Pete's sake, stop that racket," a familiar voice barked. "What's going on?" Carson Beaumont stared at Joe, his face impassive. "Oh, it's you."

"He assaulted me," Perry bleated. "He's crazy."

Carson rounded on the guy. "Perry, you're drunk, now go away and sober up." He transferred his attention back to Joe. His stony gaze traveled up and down, taking in every wrinkle and stain on Joe's clothes. Joe stared back at him. He detested Carson, but the guy was still Nina's father, and for that alone he owed him a small measure of consideration.

"I'm here to see Nina," Joe said, calm and implacable.

"Hmm." Carson glanced at the people around them, and they melted away, leaving the two of them alone. "She might have already left. Probably wants an early night, seeing as she's leaving tomorrow for Palm Springs."

The pit fell out of Joe's stomach. "Palm Springs…?"

"She's taking a job for me there."

"Oh."

His heart sank even further. So she'd had her break

from reality, and now she was ready to take up her old life. How could she still work for her father when she knew what Beaumont, Inc. had done to him? Obviously she'd gotten over that in a hurry. Just like she'd gotten over him in a hurry.

His blood felt like icy sludge in his veins. He'd driven all this way for nothing. Nothing but a proverbial kick in the gut.

Suddenly deluged with fury and humiliation, he turned away from Carson, desperate to get as far away as possible. Then, out of the corner of his eye, he glimpsed a familiar figure—a slender girl with feathery blonde hair wearing a blue dress. She was across the dance floor, sidling through the tables, the supple movements of her body so achingly familiar that his lungs seized and he couldn't breathe for a moment.

"Nina!" he choked out, and then he was striding across the dance floor, scattering couples left and right.

He hadn't been able to yell, but she appeared to hear him anyway. She spun around, and her eyes grew wide and amazed as he closed in on her.

"Joe," she breathed when he was only a couple of feet away. A pretty, dark-haired girl stood next to her. "Lindsey, this is Joe," Nina said, not taking her eyes off Joe.

"Ah, the famous Joe."

Reluctantly, Joe glanced at Nina's friend. "I'm famous?"

"Well, to me you are." Lindsey pecked Nina on the cheek. "I'm leaving now. Call me if you want. Anytime."

Nina waited until they were alone before she drew in a deep breath. "What are you doing here?"

He didn't answer her right away because first he had to drink in his fill of her. Even though she was leaving, even though she didn't love him, that didn't kill his need for her. Since she'd been gone, he'd missed her every second of every day, and after tonight he wouldn't see her again. This was his last chance.

She was dazzling in a blue silk dress that hugged her small breasts and brought out the creamy smoothness of her skin. Her hair was artfully mussed, and makeup accentuated her deep blue eyes and generous lips. But despite the polish, she didn't look all that happy. There were faint shadows beneath her eyes and a sad droop to her lips. The realization gave him a faint throb of hope. Maybe she'd missed him too?

"I came because—because—" He rubbed the back of his neck. "Because I need to apologize to you."

"A-apologize…for what?"

"Last week when I found out who you were, I was mad at you. I felt you'd duped me, and well, I'm a proud man." He took a sorely needed breath. "But not too proud to admit I overreacted. You were right. When I found out who you were, I treated you differently, and you didn't deserve that. You'd already proved yourself to me, and I should have seen that instead of lashing out because of my wounded pride. I'm sorry, Nina. Will you accept my apology?"

She looked so stunned that it was a while before she managed a nod. "Of course. I never set out to dupe anyone. I was just so sick of being a Beaumont."

He nodded. "You mentioned that before. But you never told me what it was that finally made you snap."

"Why don't we sit down?" She gestured to an empty table in a quiet corner. "We might be here for a while."

He didn't mind that. They sat on opposite sides of the table.

Nina began to tell him about the events that led to her abandoning her identity. She told him about her job, the unexpected promotion, and what her coworkers thought of her. Joe found himself growing angry on her behalf, especially when she revealed that her father had indeed organized the promotion for her. Didn't anyone see the hardworking Nina who didn't ask for any favors?

"So you just decided to stop off in Hartley?" he asked.

"Not exactly. Hartley happened because of a duck."

He blinked at her. "A duck?"

"Yeah, a duck. I was driving around a corner and there it was right in the middle of the road. I swerved to avoid it and landed my car in water in some disused quarry."

Joe caught his breath. He knew that quarry. The water was deep and dangerous. That explained the duckweed he'd seen in her hair the day they met. Thank God she'd survived. He made to reach for her hand but stopped himself.

"All I had was my phone," Nina continued. "It seemed fate was giving me a chance to be someone else, someone ordinary. So I swapped my clothes for some I found on a clothesline and walked into town, where you mistook me for someone else."

So much had happened since that first day they'd met.

"I don't think you'll ever be ordinary."

She made a moue with her lips. "How is everyone in Hartley?"

"Good. I donated the clothes you left back to the thrift store. Mrs. Stewart was very sorry to hear you'd left. She wanted you to know that the charity stall made a huge profit, thanks to some French dresses."

Her eyes grew misty, and she seemed to choke up.

He scrubbed a hand across his face as his heart began to beat faster. He'd come all this way to bare his soul to Nina, and even though she obviously didn't share his sentiments, he was going to tell her anyway, because he had to get it off his chest, and what did he have to lose, anyway, if she was leaving tomorrow?

"Nina, I didn't come here only to apologize. I came here to…to…" He shifted in his seat, aware that he was suddenly perspiring with stress.

She sat up, tense, her eyes glued on him. "Yes, Joe?" she whispered, and the husky uncertainty in her voice gave him the final spurt of courage he needed.

"I came here to tell you how I feel about you." His throat constricted, and for a moment he was unable to talk. Nina's face tightened; she seemed to be holding her breath.

"I love you, Nina." The words rushed out of him in a flood. He blinked; she blinked.

"I'm sorry, can you say that again, please?" Tiny dots of pink appeared in her cheeks.

"I'm in love with you," he slowly pronounced, his heart booming with each word. *What a relief to let it out.* All week the truth had been building up in him, and finally he could let it go like an avalanche.

The dots of pink spread across her cheeks. She looked so adorable, so beautiful. But he wouldn't allow himself to reach out and hold her hands because he knew she didn't feel the same way. He wasn't going to let this become heavy and awkward. He'd treat it like some harmless fun.

"Yeah, it's hilarious, isn't it?" he said as a slow smile widened her lips and her eyes began to dance. "Me, the 'no relationships' guy, falling for a girl in just a few weeks. But don't worry. I'm not here to ask you to run away with me or anything."

Her gorgeous smile stuttered away. "But…why not?"

He faked a nonchalant shrug. "Because I know you have other priorities. I know you're leaving for Palm Springs tomorrow." The relief he'd felt at unburdening himself faded away. Why did he love the one woman he couldn't have? Why did he love her despite knowing what she was doing?

"Oh." Nina looked down at her hands, all the light in her face dimming.

He ached for her. "Nina," he said urgently. "Don't go to Palm Springs. Don't work for your father. You deserve better than that. Go somewhere else, find another job, change your name if you have to. I know you, Nina Summers. You can succeed on your own. You don't need to stick with your dad."

She stared at him with dazed eyes. "But I have to. So that you can—"

"Have to?" He frowned at her. "Why? What does he have over you?" Then, the truth dawned sickeningly on him. "Wait. Are you going to Palm Springs in exchange for your dad not hounding me to sell anymore?"

She nodded, quiet, and Joe wanted to explode.

"How can he do that to you? And why the hell are you letting him! You're not afraid of him. Why don't you tell him to shove it?"

He was quivering with outrage, but she just sat there, big eyes fixed on him. "You can't guess why, Joe?" A nervous smile tweaked at her lips.

He stared at her, too afraid to move as another truth hit him. "Oh my God. You love me, too."

"Yes, you big dope," she choked out.

The truth shone from her eyes, filling him with light. Tentative, afraid he was imagining this, he reached both hands across the table, and she met him halfway and curled her fingers around his. Her fingers were cold and trembling, but the love glowing in her face was hot and strong.

"I am a dope," he said. "When your dad told me you were still working for him, I thought that meant you condoned his bullying tactics."

She shook her head vehemently. "I was furious with him, and I told him exactly how I felt. You need to know that Perry worked on his own to put the squeeze on the banks and use your grandmother as leverage. But that doesn't excuse my dad. And he wouldn't stop pursuing you unless I agreed to continue working for him."

She sighed in resignation, and the soft sound nearly tore Joe in two. "There's no way in hell I'm letting you work for him."

"But I want your B&B to succeed. And I don't want a megaresort spoiling Hartley." She shrugged. "Besides, I only agreed to the Palm Springs job. It'll be six months, tops."

But he knew she was just putting on a brave front. "You'll hate it. You hate it already. Admit it."

She played with his fingers, and every touch sent warmth spinning through his veins. He gazed at her with growing awe. This spunky, sassy, sexy woman was in love with him, and even if their future was uncertain, one thing was clear. Before daybreak tomorrow they would find a quiet room to be alone, where they would forget about their problems and make love until they both couldn't move.

Desire simmered in him as he eyed the outline of her breasts beneath the delicate silk. It had been too long since he'd felt her body sliding against his…

"Joe, pay attention." Nina squeezed his fingers. "Stop staring at my breasts."

He grinned at her. "I can't help it."

She wriggled in her seat, and he knew she was getting aroused, too. "I might have a solution to our problem."

Do you live close by? he wanted to quip, but instead he nodded. "Yes?"

"You need a chunk of money to get your B&B up and running. I just happen to have some spare cash to invest. Seems like a no-brainer to me."

He instantly drew his hands away from hers. "No way. I'm not taking money from you. Nope. Not gonna happen."

"Didn't you hear me? I'm not giving you the money, I'm *investing* it. Big difference."

He sat back, still stunned by her offer. "But why?"

"Don't you get it, Joe? I want to come back and settle for good in Hartley."

"You do?"

"Yes, I really do. I want to build this bed-and-breakfast with you. I want it to be the best for miles around. I want to work until my muscles ache, and then I want to go home to your house and make love to you until your muscles ache, too. And I want to drink beer at the Comet with Vince and eat Sarah's yummy food and visit your nonna and yak with Mrs. Stewart and jump into the sea with you every now and then."

It sounded like a dream. An impossible dream, but boy, did he want to believe in it.

"Won't you get bored?"

"Not if you wear those fancy pink rubber gloves every

once in a while."

"I'm serious," he said, despite holding back a chuckle at the memory of the day they met. "Won't you miss your city life, your friends and family?"

She shrugged lightly. "I'll want to visit them, sure. So what?"

She made everything sound so easy and right and do-able. If he let his imagination run free, he could see them working together as partners, relaxing as friends, pleasuring each other as lovers. In the near future he could even see himself getting down on one knee and asking her to marry him. Nina was the only woman he could imagine in his life, taking over his life.

He had to trust in her love. Had to risk his heart, everything, if he wanted her. And God, how he wanted her.

He stood and rounded the table to stand beside her, hands held out to her. "We'll have to draw up a watertight agreement."

An irresistible smile spread across her face as she clasped his hands and rose to stand in front of him. "Whatever you say, sweetheart."

Sweetheart. She'd called him sweetheart. He felt ten feet tall.

"We'll work out the exact amount needed and not a dollar more."

"Of course."

"The bed-and-breakfast will be strictly business between us, okay?"

Expressive blue eyes glimmered at him through her lashes. "Sure, Joe. Strictly business. I'll only strip naked and go skinny-dipping in the ocean when you're not around.

Promise."

Blood pounded in his veins and shot southward. He really needed to get her alone, fast.

"We might negotiate a separate contract covering skinny-dipping," he said, sounding strangled.

Laughing with delight, she wrapped her arms around his neck and hugged him. "It's going to be fun negotiating that contract. You'll be surprised what this maid can squeeze out of you!"

His millionaire maid would never cease to surprise him, of that Joe was convinced. He lowered his mouth to hers, eager for the negotiations to begin.

Acknowledgments

What would I do without my editors to guide and shape my book? Huge thanks to Stacy Abrams and Lydia Sharp for showing me how to improve this story!

About the Author

Coleen Kwan has been a bookworm all her life. At school, English was her favorite subject, but for some reason she decided on a career in IT. After many years of programming, she wondered what else there was in life — and discovered writing. She loves writing contemporary romance and steampunk romance.

Coleen lives in Sydney with her partner and two children. When she isn't writing she enjoys avoiding housework, eating chocolate and watching *The Office*.